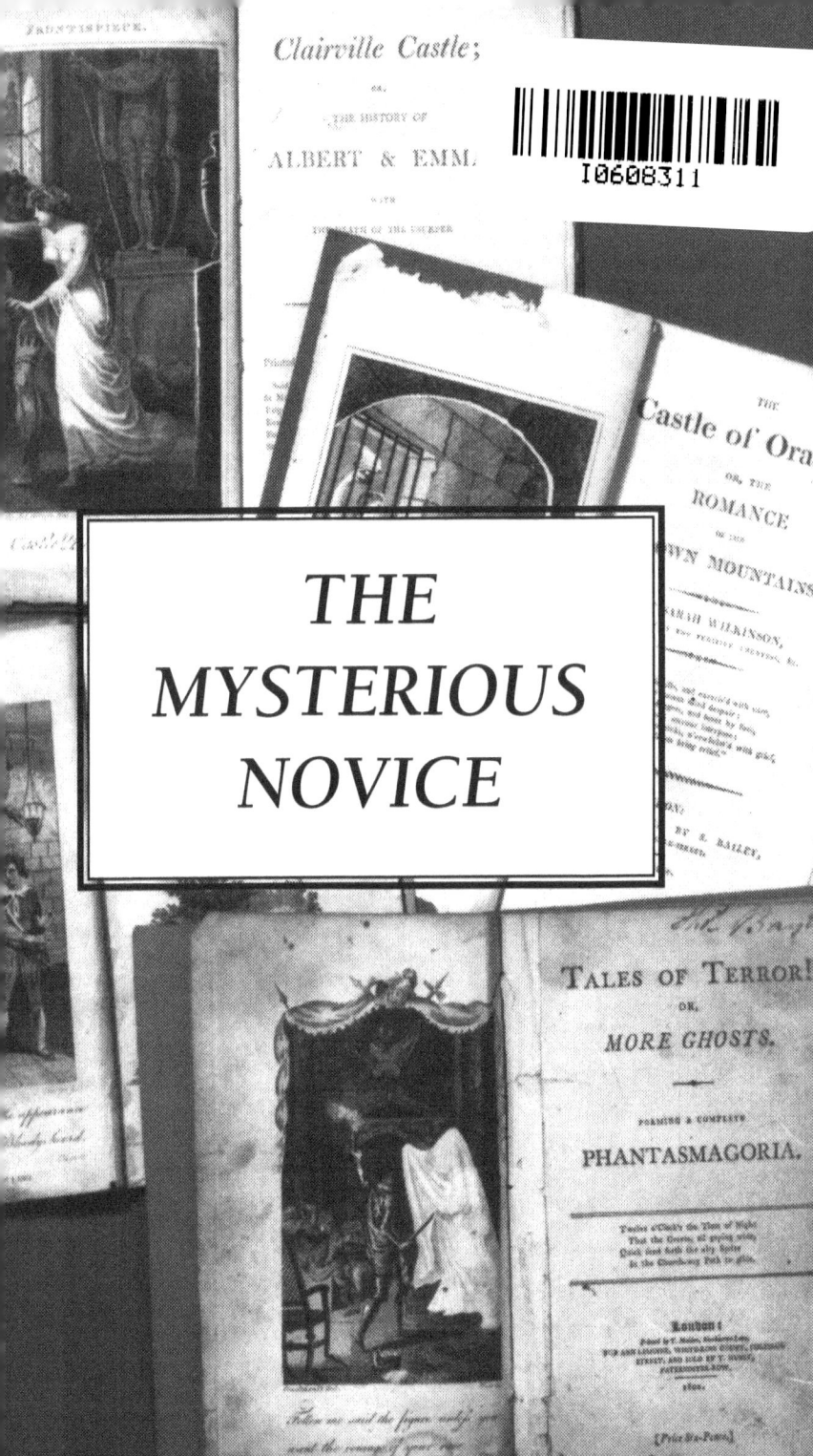

Clairville Castle;

or,

THE HISTORY OF

ALBERT & EMMA

THE Castle of Ora

or, the

ROMANCE

of the

WN MOUNTAINS

THE MYSTERIOUS NOVICE

TALES OF TERROR!

or,

MORE GHOSTS.

FORMING A COMPLETE

PHANTASMAGORIA.

THE
MYSTERIOUS
NOVICE

Stories of Terror from
the Gothic Bluebooks

Compiled and Introduced
by Peter Haining

the apocryphile press
BERKELEY, CA
www.apocryphile.org

apocryphile press
BERKELEY, CA

Apocryphile Press
1700 Shattuck Ave #81
Berkeley, CA 94709
www.apocryphile.org

First published in 1978 by the Garden City Press,
Limited in the UK. Apocryphile Press Edition, 2007.
Selection and original material ©1978 by Peter Haining.

Printed in the United States of America
ISBN 1-933993-31-6

"It must be remembered that these little 'bluebooks' were sold in their hundreds for a tester apiece, and the reason why now examplars are of the very last rarity, and good clean copies will sometimes fetch as many pounds as they were sold for pence, lies in the fact that they were read and read on every side by schoolboys, by prentices, by servant-girls, by the whole of that vast population which longed to be in the fashion, to steep themselves in the Gothic romance—but the circulating library was too expensive or inaccessible for them, and so the Gothic chapbook passed from hand to hand and was literally read to pieces. Even if a virgin copy or two by some chance survived, they would not have been for a moment deemed worthy of the bookshelf, or even of a cardboard cover. They were thrown out contemptuously; the babies crawling over the nursery floor were allowed to play with them for the sake of the pretty painted pictures, and little hands soon had them in scraps and tatters. So what were thought rubbish by our grand-mothers have become unique treasures today, a thing which is no new phenomenon in the annals of bibliography."

MONTAGUE SUMMERS
The Gothic Quest (1938)

ACKNOWLEDGEMENTS

The material included in this anthology has been obtained from the author's own collection of Gothic 'bluebooks' and those of the British Library, the University of London and the New York Public Library—and he is grateful to the staffs of those institutions for their help during his research. He has also received considerable assistance from the staff of the London Library while studying the history of English literature in the eighteenth and nineteenth centuries, and is similarly indebted to David Philips for allowing him access to his remarkable collection of Gothic publications. Thanks are also due to Mrs Elizabeth Poole who so efficiently retyped many of the original stories and, finally, Miss Livia Gollancz who supported the project from its inception.

P.H.

CONTENTS

ILLUSTRATIONS

(Between pages 116-123)

Crude illustration ftom "The Monk; Or, Father Innocent, Abbot of the Capuchins" a chapbook plagiarism of Matthew Lewis's "The Monk." Thomas Tegg, 1803.

"The Victim of Monkish Cruelty," a typical engraving from another of Thomas Tegg's popular 'Shilling Shockers' (1803).

An ill-used 'bluebook' heroine in the inevitable state of disarray — from "The Distressed Nun" by Isaac Crookenden (1802).

The discovery of the imprisoned nun, Constance, in "The Mysterious Novice" by Sarah Wilkinson (1809).

A bandit captain confronted by the beautiful ghost of one of his victims: the frontispiece to "New Collection of Gothic Stories" (1801).

A sword-waving skeleton—one of the ghastly figures found in "The Black Forest; Or, The Cavern of Horrors" (1802).

The vampire strikes! The frontispiece for "The Bride of the Isles" (circa 1820), which is credited to Lord Byron.

INTRODUCTION

IN THE YEAR 1803 the young Percy Bysshe Shelley and some of his schoolfriends at Sion House had developed one of those secretive occupations so beloved of the young—in this instance the surreptitious reading of what were termed 'bluebooks'. Unobserved, the boys would sit for hours in the shadow of some rose bushes in the school grounds devouring these forbidden volumes which they obtained from a small, rather seedy circulating library in nearby Brentford. Apart from the vicarious thrills provided by such 'horrid' material (as the boys liked to describe it), these publications had the added attraction of being cheap to loan—less than a penny each—and particularly convenient because of their size for slipping into the pocket should one of the schoolmasters suddenly appear!

Shelley, and doubtless his friends too, never forgot the excitement provided by these little books, and certainly many authorities have seen their influence in his early writings. Nor were they the only ones who enjoyed them: hundreds of thousands of men, women and young people of all classes were eager customers of the multitude of titles which flowed from a host of publishers. Yet today, nearly two centuries later, the 'bluebook' phenomena is forgotten almost as if it never existed: ignored in most works about eighteenth- and nineteenth-century literature and only briefly appraised in studies of the Gothic novel. Even seventy years ago, Thomas Medwin, Shelley's biographer, who recounted his subject's youthful pleasure with the books in *The Life of Percy Bysshe Shelley* (1913), felt his readers *ought* to know what they were, but nonetheless explained:

"Who does not know what bluebooks mean? But if there should be anyone ignorant enough not to know what those dear, darling volumes, so designated from their covers, contains, be it known, that they are or were to be bought for sixpence, and embodied stories of haunted castles, bandits, murderers, and other grim personages—a most exciting and interesting food for boys' minds."

The 'bluebooks' were, to be precise, a whole range of publications which had appeared to satisfy the craze for Gothic literature which had been developed a few years earlier by the novels of Horace Walpole, Ann Radcliffe and Matthew 'Monk' Lewis. As the reader is no doubt aware, tales and legends of terror had been part of man's heritage from the very earliest times, but it was the emergence of the Gothic novel during the oppressive and uneasy last decade of the eighteenth century which had caused a "Renaissance of wonder" and thereby established a literary genre which has continued to the present day. In two previous volumes, *Great British Tales of Terror* and *Great Tales of Terror from Europe and America* (Gollancz, 1972; Penguin Books, 1973),* I studied the development of the genre during the years 1756 to 1840, and by including stories from many of the most famous writers and important books, was able to show how their work was the forerunner of the modern literature of the macabre. This book complements those previous volumes in that it gives similar treatment to the other strata of Gothic publishing then taking place.

The Gothic novels were, of course, mostly very long and without exception expensive: far beyond the slender pockets of the average man and woman—and schoolboys, for that matter. Yet as always when a public interest such as this develops, there are invariably those who are ready to see that it reaches the hands of the masses in some form or other. In his excellent study, *The Gothic Quest* (1938), Montague Summers, the leading historian of the genre, explains how easy it was to satisfy the demand:

"The Gothic novel, a lengthy affair, in its four volumes or three volumes, as the case might be, was abridged, compressed and imitated upon a small scale, and the cheaper presses began to pour out in undiminished spate legions upon legions of 'bluebooks' which were the lineal descendants of the earlier chapbooks, and which were bought in infinity by exactly the same class of purchaser."

---

* In the U.S., these works are available as a single volume entitled *Gothic Tales of Terror* (Taplinger, 1972; Penguin Books, 1973). The story of horror literature following the Gothic era is continued in *The Penny Dreadful*, ed. Peter Haining (Gollancz, 1975).

The concept was undoubtedly simplicity itself: but it would be wrong to think the 'bluebooks' were merely miniature versions of the originals. The folk of town and country, many semi-literate, wanted more than just the leisurely storytelling and often convoluted plots of the Gothic novels. But this had been thought of, too, as Montague Summers again tells us: "It was the aim of the writer of the 'bluebook' first to give his narrative as exciting a title as possible; secondly to cram into his limited space as many shocking, mysterious and horrid incidents as possible."

In Summers's description lies the clue as to how the publications earned their more evocative appellation of 'Shilling Shockers', although, as we shall see, a shilling was not necessarily always the price. Let another expert who has handled many copies of these now increasingly rare items, and well understands their appeal, put the matter more fully. He is William W. Watt, writing in an essay, "Shilling Shockers of the Gothic School", published in 1932:

Like most of the books of bygone days, [Mr. Watt explains] the 'Shilling Shockers' are as interesting in their external appearance as in their content. They were about four by seven inches in size, and their closely printed pages were poorly stitched into a cover of flimsy blue paper. The stories varied in length from mere anecdotes to tales of thirty thousand words, but many of the publishers specialised in definite lengths, dealing out thirty-six pages for sixpence and seventy-two for a shilling. The nameless authors, confined within limits like modern newspaper columnists, were often obliged to bring the hero and heroine to the grave or the altar with surprising suddenness, or, vice versa, to create near the end new characters and incidents with only the faintest possible links to the main story, in order to give the reader his money's worth of thrills. Often, when a story fell short of its quota, the remaining pages were filled in with an additional anecdote. . . . Many of the shockers were anthologies of shorter tales.

Perhaps, though, *the* most important element in attracting the basically unsophisticated readership, was the engraved frontispiece which faced the title page. These pictures, occasionally daubed with red, yellow, blue and green colours, invariably showed some sensational incident such as a frightened and bare-bosomed girl threatened by a grinning monk or evil spectre; a dark and gloomy hero in the clutches of a group of bandits; or a frowning villain about to hurl his victim over a precipice or castle battlements. The impact of these pictures was heightened all the more by their proximity to such appealing double-barrelled titles as "The Secret Oath; Or, The Blood Stained Dagger", "The Miseries of Miranda; Or, The Cavern of Horror" and "Nocturnal Visits; Or, The Mysterious Husband". The frequent combination of 'love interest' and 'horrid' elements in the titles also proved irresistible. (A variation of this technique can, of course, still be seen flourishing today in the best-selling paperback 'Gothic Romances' which are so popular among women readers on both sides of the Atlantic.)

In fairness, it has to be said that many 'bluebooks' promised more than they delivered: and the more unscrupulous publishers ("the parasitic presses of Houndsditch, and the Borough and Finsbury Square" as Summers calls them) were not above including illustrations of dramatic moments that never occurred in the stories at all. Nor of giving them titles which bore scant relation to the text. Yet, the general public then—as now—lived in eager expectation and were easily and often parted from their sixpences and shillings.

Of course, publishers and writers plagiarised the popular works which had caused their being, quite unmercifully (even on occasions appropriating authors' names for totally scurrilous works) and the likes of Ann Radcliffe and Matthew Lewis—unprotected as they then were by any form of copyright—saw their novels appearing in abridged, extracted or imitated form in many of the 'bluebooks'. One need only study a copy of the anonymous "The Midnight Assassin; Or, Confessions of the Monk Rinaldi" (1802) to find it is an abridgement of Mrs Radcliffe's *The Italian; Or, The Confessional of the Black Penitents* (1797), while the similarly uncredited "Almagro and Claude; Or, Monastic Murder" (1803) is a none-too-subtle version of Lewis's *The Monk* (1796). No doubt in the light of this wholesale piracy it is not surprising that most of the 'bluebook' writers remained anonymous and we only know the names of a very few of them.

Because so many of these flimsy publications have long since disappeared it is quite impossible to tell just how many were copies of their Gothic forebears—or, on the other hand, how many were genuine originals. It has been suggested that because many of the 'Shilling Shocker' plots are so complicated, it is difficult to believe they were conceived on any scale but that of a full-length novel, and must therefore be plagiarisms. This apart, it is possible to find in many of them the two major themes which dominated the Gothic genre: dark deeds in a monastery or convent (*vide The Monk* and *The Italian*) and the haunted castle (Walpole's *The Castle of Otranto*, etc.). While other stock situations are also there in abundance: abduction, rescue, seduction and villainy; secret passages and missing manuscripts; thwarted lovers and distressed maidens; ducal fathers and wicked barons; bandits, ghosts, lecherous monks and treacherous nuns. Plus, of course—unchanging through all adversity—the beautiful heroine with her unblemished virtue and ability to swoon at the first sight or sound of anything 'horrid'.

Only the young hero is in a different mould, as William Watt informs us: "The young hero was a relatively unimportant character in the outstanding Gothic novels, because Walpole, Mrs Radcliffe and Lewis, realising that vice was far more alluring to their readers than virtue, emphasised the portrayal of the dark villain, evolving that curious hybrid between heroism and villainy which later came to be known as the 'Byronic hero'. In the shilling shockers, however, the virtuous young hero, contrasted with the decidedly unheroic villain at last comes into his own."

Naturally, because of all these characteristics, it is easy to write off the whole 'bluebook' phenomenon as derivative and crude. Devendra P. Varma, in *The Gothic Flame* (1957), takes a disparaging viewpoint shared by a number of other experts when he writes, "The stories provided nothing original. The 'love interest' was subordinated to the thrill-producing machinery; they clung to certain conventions of Gothic plot; and the characters were exaggerated to an astonishing degree.... Their publication and commercial value stand as an index of the sensation-craze into which the Gothic vogue degenerated in its declining years."

This is not a view that I can accept—nor do I share Varma's belief that the 'bluebooks' only "catered to the perverted taste for excitement among degenerate readers"! For my research has not only unearthed some important and clearly original material in these publications, but increased a long-held conviction that they are the seeds from which the modern horror short story flowered. It is a view also shared by no less an authority than Professor Edith Birkhead who says in her study, *The Tale of Terror* (1921):

"It is in these brief, blood-curdling romances that we may find the origin of the short tale of terror, which became so popular a form of literature in the nineteenth century. . . . It was probably the success of the chapbook that encouraged the editors of periodicals early in the nineteenth century to enliven their pages with sensational fiction."

Even Montague Summers has admitted that "occasionally the 'bluebook' was to some extent original" and perhaps if he had had the time, during his herculean labours in the Gothic field, to examine more of the publications, he might have made the statement with greater emphasis. Certainly during my study of the 'golden years' of the 'Shilling Shockers'—which extended from 1800 to 1820—I have been able to locate a number of items which considerably extend our knowledge and, I believe, our appreciation of the genre. For example, one of them published what was in all probability the first short story to feature a man-into-beast werewolf; while a second is devoted entirely to one of the very earliest vampire tales—set in Scotland of all places! To them add a unique American witchcraft story taking a sceptical view of the subject, a legend that may well have played a part in the creation of Mary Shelley's classic horror novel, *Frankenstein,* and an item which can really have no other categorisation than pioneer science fiction!

Not that my collection ends there: for balance I felt it was important to include a few very typical items about monks, nuns, bandits and ghosts—not to mention hard-pressed heroes and heroines—to represent what was after all the vast majority of 'bluebook' material, and in so doing enable the reader to see what so enthralled his forebears. Taken all together, the stories present as full a picture of the range of the 'Shilling Shockers' as I think it is possible to get at this late date. In any event, I believe the combination of the expected and the unexpected will reveal these neglected and mostly forgotten publications in a new light to historian and general reader alike.

Even if, in the final analysis, the 'bluebooks' only showed real ingenuity and originality in a comparatively few instances, they did, I am convinced, establish something else most important just by their presence—a bridge between the lengthy Gothic novels and the short story of terror. As William Watt has also observed: "The 'Shilling Shockers' went out of existence about 1820, but their place was taken by the monthly magazines, and the tradition of terror was ably carried on in the tales and short stories of Scott, Bulwer-Lytton, and Wilkie Collins in England, and Irving, Hawthorne and Poe in America." (On the larger scale, of course, the Gothic novel led to the Romantic Revival and with it the glorious works of Byron, Shelley, Coleridge, Goethe, Schiller and many more.)

It would, I am sure, be impossible to expect that the modern reader, like Henry Tilney in *Northanger Abbey*, will find himself devouring the stories which follow with his "hair standing on end all the time". Yet, I do believe he will find them intriguing, often exciting and each and every one fascinating as a precursor of the modern short story of the macabre. For those reasons alone, they have been worth rescuing from oblivion.

1

THE VINDICTIVE MONK

Or, The Fatal Ring

by Isaac Crookenden

Certainly the most sensational of all Gothic horror novels was Matthew Lewis's *The Monk* which appeared in 1796 and was almost immediately the centre of a storm of controversy and outrage. Prior to the publication of this remarkable novel about a young friar who allows himself to be tempted into a life of lechery and concourse with the devil, the Gothic novel had concerned itself with haunted castles and derring-do of one kind or another. Lewis's book "rioted in horrors to an extent hardly to be found elsewhere", according to a contemporary critic, and there were soon determined attempts by several authorities to have it banned on the grounds it was blasphemous and obscene. Indeed, the charges against Lewis grew so fierce that he felt compelled to expurgate certain scenes of seduction and diabolism from later editions. Nonetheless, the book made Lewis (1775–1818) the literary lion of England, and whatever may have been the shortcomings of the story, it undoubtedly played a major part in establishing the horror genre—and its influence can still be felt today in successful book/films like *Rosemary's Baby* and *The Exorcist*. Not surprisingly, *The Monk* was seized on early in the development of the 'Shilling Shocker', and in the first few years of the nineteenth century was abridged, extracted and plagiarised countless times by 'bluebook' writers and publishers. One of the few writers of this school who is known to us by name, Isaac Crookenden, utilised the theme in several of his works, but attempted to be more original with the idea in "The Vindictive Monk; Or, The Fatal Ring", one of a collection of 'horrid' short stories published under the delightfully innocuous title, *Romantic Tales*, by S. Fisher of St John Lane,

Clerkenwell, in 1802. Although we know little of Crookenden, except that he wrote tirelessly for several publishers like Fisher, he displays several of the qualities which were later to make writers of short horror stories popular, and provides a fascinating picture of the kind of unprincipled monk who was such a favourite character in the 'bluebooks'.

*   *   *

THE YOUNG CALINI was descended of a good family and heir to great and still-increasing wealth. He was the last representative of an honourable house, and the delight and admiration not only of his doting parents, but of everybody who knew him. He possessed every grace of mental perfection; for his education had been conducted on so liberal a plan, that a clear, just, and accurate perception had been the happy result of his juvenile studies. His person was in every way answerable to the above delineation of his mind. His make exhibited the truest symmetry; and his countenance beamed with masculine dignity, corrected with a gracious condescension.

Although Calini was reared in the principles of the Romanist Church, that did not hinder him from seeing some of its absurdities; and therefore, while some of the votaries placed the essence of their religion in a gaudy exhibition of pompous ceremonies, his consisted in a steady, uniform system of good actions; an undeviating rectitude of conduct, prompted by the motive of his present and everlasting interest, as well as by the intrinsic beauty of benevolence. Such was the youth, whom we have selected for the hero of these memoirs.

One day his father (as the youth had ever considered him), took him aside, and spoke as follows—

"The substance of what I am going to unfold, I once thought I should have buried in oblivion; but, upon mature deliberation, I am come to a determination of entrusting you with it. You have always been thought to be my son. This is the moment to undeceive you. You are *not* my child!"—"Not your son!" exclaimed the youth, in the utmost astonishment; "whose then can I be?"— "That you will never probably know," replied Signor Calini. "But you have not many obligations to your parents, who left you to

perish in your infancy. My story excites your astonishment. Listen
attentively, while I disclose the circumstance which induced me to
bring you up as my own offspring. About twenty years ago, as
I was landing from a gondola, one dark night, on the northern
shores of the Adriatic, after I had returned from visiting one of
my estates, my sight was struck with a white bundle within a foot
from the waves; on examining which, I found it contained an infant. It was yourself; and I resolved that the direful intentions
of those who left you should not only be frustrated, but I would
adopt you as my son, two of mine having recently died. When I
got home, I examined the bundle more accurately, and was surprised to see this ring." (Here he presented one to the astonished
youth.) "You see, it is of a peculiar make; there is some name
underneath." (The young man turned it, and saw the word
Ollorini engraved on it.) "I beg, that from this day you would
wear it, to remind you of the singular event; and be assured, my
dear boy, although you are not the natural issue of my own loins,
yet I shall always feel for you a father's tenderness."

Here Signor Calini concluded his narration, and left his auditor
overwhelmed with astonishment. The barbarity of his real parents
affected him severely; but the kindness of the Signor afforded him
a continual source of the most pleasing sensation.

A short time after this wondrous disclosure, young Calini (for
so we shall still call him) had been to visit a young lady, to whom
he was sincerely attached; and was now returning home on horse-
back. The night was far advanced, and very threatening. His road
lay through a dark wood, in the midst of which, he was seized by
two men, who dragged him along, until they came to the ruins of
an old castle. Here they halted, and one, who had a lamp, sought
for a door, and at length told his comrade he had found it. They
then led our hero through a long intricate passage, at the end of
which they unbolted a heavy iron door, and entered a gloomy stone
dungeon. A strong chain, which was fastened to an enormous staple
in the wall, discovered to the youth the horrors which awaited him.
"Here," said one of the ruffians, "here is your habitation, till
you resign all pretensions to Lady Alexa." Our young lover now
saw through the whole affair. He had been seized by order of a
rival; but who this rival was, he had no means of judging. The
inhuman monsters chained him to the wall, and, without speaking

another word, left the dungeon. This mysterious event we shall now unfold.

There lived, in the neighbourhood of Calini, a monk called Sceloni; of a gloomy character, and who was never seen once to smile. He was dependent on a nobleman, and had, from motives of self-interest, engaged to administer to his lewd propensities. This nobleman was enamoured of the very same lady our hero loved. Seeing no possibility of supplanting him in her affection, he called in the aid of the dark Sceloni, to whom he promised great pecuniary rewards, if he would dispatch his rival, and secure to him the possession of Alexa. The avaricious Italian undertook to perform what he required. For this purpose, he waylaid the youth on his return from Alexa's house, as we have observed. But as he did not wish to embrue his hands in blood, if it could be done without, he had conveyed him to the ruins of the castle, whose intricate windings he well knew. Here he meant to keep him, till he should be able to extort an oath from him, that he would for ever resign all pretensions to Alexa. When he left the dungeon, he went directly to his employer, and told him the rival of his love was removed beyond the possibility of again being formidable. Signor Holbruzi took these words to mean no less than the death of the youth; and therefore the monk reaped the golden reward he aimed at.

But, notwithstanding this, Alexa was decidedly against his suit; and as she could not but be surprised at Calini's unaccountable absence, as well as very much affected at it, she not only conceived additional disgust at Holbruzi's addresses, but began to be suspicious of some base design having been executed against Calini. In the meantime, that unfortunate youth was suffering the severest extremities of imprisonment, and calling in vain on his dear Alexa. He was visited in the dungeon frequently by the monk, Sceloni, who endeavoured, by every means in his power, to make him resign all pretensions to Alexa; but he was steady in his refusal; nor did he yield, even when he was threatened with assassination. Calini was as unsuccessful in trying to discover the name and quality of his rival, as Sceloni was in extorting a resignation of Alexa.

After Sceloni had quitted the dungeon, the miserable youth began to reflect anew on his unhappy situation. He saw no probability of being united to the beloved object of his soul; why then not resign her? There was something in this word which seemed to imply cowardice, and he pertinaciously objected to it. Holbruzi finding Alexa so little disposed to favour his passion, was resolved to possess her at all events. He ordered Sceloni to force her from her home, and bring her to his palace; which, under cover of a dark night, he effected.

Alexa was left an orphan at an early age; and, after her parents' death, she was reared up by a tender aunt, who loved her as her own child. But having a very slender income, necessity had obliged this good woman to part with an estate in Piedmont, and she had purchased a small but neat villa in the neighbourhood of Naples, where she resided with her beloved niece. The young Calini had found them out in their retirement, and had made his addresses to the fair Alexa; which at first was discouraged by the aunt, not as she had any objection to the youth; on the contrary, she was convinced he was worthy of her niece; but she knew the girl was his inferior in point of fortune. Yet when she found how firm he had taken hold of Alexa's heart, and likewise heard of the liberal sentiments of Signor Calini, she no longer opposed the mutual bias of their young and innocent hearts.

Things were in this situation, when Calini discontinued so unaccountably (to them at least) his visits. This circumstance, severe as it was to the young lady, was also felt by her aunt, who had conceived the greatest friendship for him. But her sorrows were unspeakably acute, when one night several ruffians broke into the house, and tore away her beloved Alexa. These were the cruel Sceloni and his emissaries, who conveyed her to the monster Holbruzi, as already related. But that lascivious wretch did not yet find his end answered. The persecuted maid was enabled to make a vigorous resistance to his meretricious wishes. Force he could have employed; but this he determined to delay, till every other method had been tried. He thought no way so likely to weaken her virtuous resolutions, as to let her know that her union with Calini was impossible, as that being was no longer an inhabitant of earth. This fatal intelligence overwhelmed her unfortunate breast with fresh despair, and rendered Holbruzi more than ever an object of disgust and abhorrence. His pride was severely mortified by her fixed dislike and undisguised contempt. At this unseasonable moment, Sceloni solicited a new supply for his late services in bringing Alexa to the nobleman's palace. Holbruzi, smarting with the indifference of that female, answered sternly, that his trifling services had already been more than sufficiently rewarded; and, after rebuking him sharply for his avarice, absolutely refused to give him another carlin (fourpence of our money).

The monk seemed all humility, but he quitted the palace with a soul full of revenge; to accomplish which, he concerted a deep-laid scheme. He retired to the outskirts of the city, wrote to Holbruzi that he was leaving his monastery (for this wretch was of an holy order), and going to a different part of the world; but conjured him to release the young Calini (who he confessed was alive, but imprisoned), and he described a dungeon where the youth was *not*. After he had sent this letter, he provided himself with a brace of pistols, and repaired to that very dungeon which he had mentioned in his letter as the prison of Calini. Here he threw himself on the ground, and impersonating the distress of that unfortunate youth, waited deliberately for Holbruzi's arrival; for he never doubted but that vindictive tyrant would come to sacrifice Calini with his own hand. He was not deceived in his conjecture. When that monster received the monk's letter, his countenance bespoke the savage passions it inspired. "What!" said he. "My detested rival living! This night he breathes his last." He accordingly stole away that very evening, muffled up in a disguise, with a lamp in one hand, and a dagger in the other, through the dark passages of the ruins. Sceloni heard him coming, and uttered a groan, on purpose to direct his steps to the dungeon where he was. The monk soon heard the door unfastened, and he kept his finger close to the trigger. Holbruzi cautiously advanced the light, and then entered. The subtle Sceloni lay as if he was in a disturbed sleep. Holbruzi drew near; and as he bent over him, exclaimed, "Favoured minion! Wilt thou ever more rival me in love? Thou sleepest. Awake in—" he would have said *death*, but at this moment the pseudo-Calini pressed the trigger, and dismissed his soul from this world.

But Sceloni was not yet satisfied; his revengeful soul thirsted for more blood. He considered that if Calini had resigned Alexa, that maid, out of revenge, might have yielded to Holbruzi, and consequently he should not have met with that mortifying refusal from him, which had stimulated him to take the bloody means that he had just executed. His vindictive spirit resolving upon a

double revenge, marked Calini for a second victim. No sooner
had he made his horrible determination, but, snatching up the
lamp (which had not been extinguished in falling), and the blood-
less dagger, he rushed out of the dungeon and into that of the
destined youth, fully resolved to accomplish his dreadful purpose.
The report of the pistol, as it was at a considerable distance from
young Calini, and vented in a close-pent dungeon, did not reach
his auditory nerves; and he was yet in a deep slumber, with his
right hand on his breast. Sceloni drew near to strike; but, on
observing the position of his hand, stooped down to remove it. The
rays of the light discovered the ring, which his supposed father
desired him to wear. It excited Sceloni's curiosity. He gently drew
it off, and examined it by the lamp. Each moment furnished new
alarm in his terrified mind. His face assumed an ashy paleness; his
joints trembled with amazement and horror; but when he turned
it up, and saw the engraved name of 'Ollorini' upon it, his horror
and astonishment was complete. He hastily threw away the dagger;
and awaking the youth, interrogated him about the mysterious
ring. He could only relate what his supposed father had told him.
This was enough. Sceloni, while convulsive sobs burst from his
torn bosom, could only exclaim, "I am your father." The astonished
youth looked up, and thought his reason was unsettled, but seeing
his tears and groans, he knew not what to think. At length, he
desired him to give some indubitable proof he was his father.
"I will, my son, I will do it," answered the monk, "but this is not
a proper place for conversation; let me unbind you from these
ignominious chains!" He then freed the youth from his fetters;
and they left the dungeon together, and retired to a small house,
where, after they had entered a private room, he addressed the
wondering impatient youth as follows:

"Although, in reciting these circumstances which prove you to
be my son, I must incriminate myself; yet I shall not hesitate to
do it, as I am sensible that you have more virtue than to conspire
against the life of your father." Here he paused a moment; for he
recollected, that he himself had conspired against the life of his
son. At length, he proceeded. 'My real name is Dictori. I was
brought up under very indulgent parents. My natural temper,
which was violent in the extreme, was put into a hot-bed, by the

unreasonable and fatal indulgence of those parents. 'Tis that indulgence which has caused my ruin. If they had done their duty, and restrained, by due correction, the impetuosity of my natural temper, I should not have been a prey to those destructive passions of my nature, which have since acted as gourds to prick me forward down the slippery path of vice. I was early attached to a lady, whose name was Mariana Vicenza; but my native pride was severely wounded when I discovered that she not only beheld me with indifference, but with a fixed dislike. I now, through obstinacy, advanced my suit with more eagerness than ever; when it would have been more honourable silently to withdraw it. However, her parents obliged her to accept of my hand at the altar. As I never could forgive the little affection she had shown for me, I soon began to retaliate upon her after marriage. Among other passions which I vented upon her without mercy, the demon of jealousy began to agitate my restless breast with its hydra horrors. I thought it very probable that she, who was forced to marry a man whom she did not like, should entertain in his absence one she did. My suspicions were strengthened by seeing this very ring upon her finger, which I apprehended was given her by her gallant. I went so far as to believe you were his child. In a frenzy of rage, I murdered my wife, and committed you to the waves, together with the detested and fatal ring. I have had proof since, that that very ring was given her before marriage by an uncle who had gone beyond the sea; that he had his name engraved on it, which was Ollorini. As I was afraid to stay in that part, I came to Naples, and became a monk of the order of St Francis. Spare me the rest!"

This truly wonderful relation affected the astonished youth a great deal.

But we must take leave of the monk and young Calini a little while to look after the lovely persecuted Alexa. That unfortunate maid was ready to abandon herself to despair. Torn away from her peaceful retreat by ruffians, at the dreadful, the horror-working hour of midnight, to fall a prey to the unbridled lust of a lewd barbarian! Separated from her dear aunt! Torn too from the fond, and protecting arms of the youth she sighed for! What can exceed her misery, wretched captive as she then was in the most hated mansion of the nefarious monster Holbruzi? For she as yet knew nothing of the sanguinary scenes which had been exhibited in the castle ruins. The savage Holbruzi, when he left his house at midnight, had consigned the wretched maid to one of his trusty servants, who executed with relentless rigour the confidence reposed in him. We now, for a short time, turn from the unhappy beauty, to see the mournful effect which her loss had upon her disconsolate aunt. That distressed matron, now separated by cruel fate from a beloved niece, in whom her very existence seemed to be wrapt up, experienced the most poignant anguish that can possibly be imagined. She wrung her aged hands in wild despair, and in frantic accents called on her far-off niece, her dear Alexa. While she was in the height of her lamentation, a knocking at the door was heard. For a considerable time she was afraid to open it, lest in so doing, she should let in those who ravished from her embraces her beloved niece, and thereby become herself a victim of their savage fury. But while she hesitated what to do, she heard a voice at the door requesting admission, the cadence of which she thought she remembered, though her distress would not permit her to be certain to whom it belonged. She however assumed courage sufficient to open it, at which Calini directly rushed in. As he knew nothing of Alexa being at Holbruzi's detested mansion, he, as soon as he left the monk, repaired to her residence, though not without dreadful apprehensions for her safety, occasioned by the silence of Sceloni, on his asking after her.

It may perhaps be thought strange, that the monk should not have told his son where she was; seeing he knew she was at Holbruzi's palace. But if we consider that he had been some time absent from Naples, and that he knew so much of that villain as to think it probable that he had murdered that maid, before he intended to assassinate her lover, we shall cease to wonder at his conduct. Add to this, that if he had discovered to Calini that Alexa was at Holbruzi's mansion, it would naturally have introduced an inquiry into that monster's mysterious absence—an inquiry which would doubtless have directed the finger of suspicion to himself. This was what the monk dreaded should transpire. He had already dipped his hands so deep in blood, that his conscience was always pointing to the gibbet, or the inquisitorial torture. He had therefore preserved an obstinate silence respecting Alexa; and our hero, unable to endure the tortures of suspense, flew upon the pinions of indescribable anxiety to her aunt's, as already mentioned.

When Calini asked for Alexa, all her grief was renewed; and she told the distracted lover the real truth. "Dragged away at midnight!" exclaimed our frantic hero. "I am the football of destiny. Why did I not die in my prison?" In a little time, however, he became more calm; and he vowed to discover her, if it was within the verge of possibility.

The reputed father of our hero received his foster son with the greatest joy imaginable, and heard with astonishment and horror the circumstances which had happened to him. He was, however, severely afflicted at the loss of the amiable Alexa; for that lovely maid stood very high both in his esteem and affection; and he had beheld the growing love which the youth evinced for her with cheerful approbation. It excited his utmost surprise to think who could possibly have stolen her from her peaceful home. He little thought that it was the machinations of one who often partook of his hospitality, and had been a frequent visitor at his festive board. But this very consideration enabled our hero to trace out her persecutor, and her present prison. He recollected Holbruzi being at his father's, as he then thought him; as likewise, that he was always exceedingly discourteous to himself, the occasion of which he had in vain attempted to unravel; but now it appeared plain enough. Calini considered also, that he knew perfectly well of his love for Alexa, as also the place of that young lady's residence. When therefore he, in his cooler moments, put all these circumstances together, the suspicions they excited were so strong, that our unfortunate youth found it impossible to think otherwise than that he must be certainly somehow concerned, if not a principal agent in the removal of the unfortunate girl.

Influenced by this supposition, he determined to go directly to the palace of Holbruzi, to see if the beloved of his soul was really there. But, upon second thoughts, he resolved to wait for night; and set spies in the meantime about the house, to discover, if possible, the secret transactions going forward in it. The spies brought him intelligence, that they saw a young lady superficially through one of the windows, leaning upon her arm in a melancholy posture, and that she appeared to be in extreme distress. This was sufficient to stimulate our hero to instant exertion. He directly went, with a desperate determination, well armed; resolving, if they denied him admission, to force the door. But the servant admitted him upon the first summons, expecting it was his master. Our hero instantly rushed upstairs; and hearing a female scream, he broke into the room and beheld his beloved Alexa, struggling in the embraces of a ruffian; whom he severely wounded, and rescued the lovely maid.

How she rejoiced to see her dear, her loved Calini! He now found no difficulty in being united to his dear Alexa; whose marriage was celebrated amid an amazing multitude of admiring spectators.

The monk, after this, was never seen beyond the walls of his convent; but passed his life in the most rigorous penance.

II

THE MYSTERIOUS NOVICE
Or, Convent of the Grey Penitents
by Sarah Wilkinson

If Matthew Lewis was the leader of the 'sensational' school of Gothic horror, then Mrs Ann Radcliffe (1764–1823) was certainly the leading light of the more restrained Gothic 'romance' story. Such novels were primarily concerned with beautiful heroines enmeshed in an apparently supernatural mystery—yet in these mysteries all would eventually be rationally explained and the young innocent delivered safely to the arms of her lover. Mrs Radcliffe's most famous works of this kind were *The Mysteries of Udolpho* (1794) and *The Italian; Or, The Confessional of the Black Peniten*ts (1797). In these books she displayed an ingenuity of plot and sense of narrative which made her immensely readable, and certain critics have seen her as the forerunner of the modern thriller writer. Despite her refined upbringing and sheltered, respectable married life, Mrs Radcliffe was well aware of the natural curiosity that existed among the general public about the lives of nuns, and with *The Italian*, opened the floodgates to a whole school of novels, of varying degrees of sensationalism, about convent life. It was, of course, not long since the days when fathers forced unwanted or troublesome daughters into strict religious orders for life, and the very mention of certain orders was enough to chill the reader even before he or she got past the title page. The 'Shilling Shockers' had a field day with such material, and Sarah Wilkinson, another of the few 'bluebook' writers whose name appeared on her works, was particularly adept at composing these stories. One need only turn to her "The Fugitive Countess; Or, The Convent of St Ursula" (1807) or "The Convent of the Grey Penitents; Or, The Apostate Nun"

(1810) for typical examples of her expertise. Miss Wilkinson was undeniably under the influence of Mrs Radcliffe when she wrote her first story about the Grey Penitents, "The Mysterious Novice", in 1809, and which I have reprinted here. This 'original romance' as it is described by the publisher, John Arliss of 87 Bartholomew Close, London, ran to 36 pages, sold for sixpence, and bore a striking engraving of a dramatic moment from the story of the luckless Constance, the incarcerated nun of the Grey Penitents, which is reproduced later in the book.

*   *   *

THE DEEP TOLLING of the convent bell announced the decease of the Madre Vitoria Ursula, an abbess of the rigid order of Grey Penitents. This event, though long expected, was a source of unfeigned sorrow and regret to the sisterhood. Though vested by the rules of the foundation with an almost despotic sway, she had tempered her authority with tenderness and benevolence. Her deportment, though mild and affable, had a dignity of expression, that prevented undue familiarity from those committed to her charge, and procured respect.

This amiable woman had just attained her forty-second year, when her eyelids were closed by death. To her it had no terror; she trusted in the mercy of that Being, with whom she hoped her peace was made. Her errors had long been renounced and repented of. One person alone she had in her younger days seriously injured; to her she had made every reparation that lay within her power, but her fault was never forgiven. Every year, instead of weakening the rancour of her enemy, appears to have added strength to the most deadly hate, that ever lodged within a female breast.

Among the novices belonging to the convent, was an interesting young woman, named Constance; she had been a peculiar favourite of the late abbess, and now mourned her loss in a manner that showed the sincerity of her anguish. The affection and solicitude the abbess displayed in every thing relative to Constance, was the only instance of preference or partiality that had occurred during her superintendence of the convent; to the others, she was ever uniformly kind and just. For several days previous to the death of the Madre, Constance had been almost her only companion and attendant, she sat up with her every night; but during those lonely hours the presence of one or other of the lay sisters was always requested. When the last hour of the abbess' life arrived, she received the sacred rites of the church from the hands of the holy Father Francis, who gave her a solemn benediction and retired; according to their rules, the whole of the sisterhood were assembled around the bed to witness the awful scene; with one hand the dying sufferer grasped a small silver crucifix, the other was held by the weeping Constance, till the moment that her excellent friend ceased to breathe. Her last gaze was fixed on the lovely novice; and, as she expired, she uttered the word 'Remember'. Constance was going to reply, but perceiving that the abbess had quitted this earthly state, she fainted in the arms of Agnes, a lay sister, who stood next her, and was borne insensible to her cell.

The new abbess did not arrive at the convent till a fortnight subsequent to the interment of her predecessor had passed. She came from a Neapolitan convent; it being the rules of the Grey Penitents not to choose an abbess from among their own sisterhood, but to have one nominated by the presiding bishop. The present superior numbered a few years more than the late abbess had done, yet she appeared healthy, robust, and much elevated with her new dignity. She belonged to the same convent as her predecessor, and it appeared that great interest had been made by her friends to get her the succession. When Constance was informed that the Duke di Beroces' daughter, the Lady Josephina, was the new abbess, she gave a convulsive start and had nearly fainted; three of the nuns were present, among whom was sister Clara, a woman of repulsive manners, artful, penetrating, and apt to put malicious constructions on the most innocent events. For this well-known disposition, she had rendered herself an object of dislike to the late superior; who treated her with civility, but never admitted her to the least share in her confidential concerns. Clara perceived the emotions of Constance with surprise, and eagerly enquired why the mention of the new abbess caused such agitation? The novice replied, that the thoughts of her late friend forcibly recurred to her mind, and she felt it would give her pain to congratulate her successor, however amiable she might be. The other sisters appeared satisfied with this explanation, and praised her sensibility; but Clara retired with a look expressive of incredulity.

The chapel, for the space of a month, was hung with black, in respect to the memory of the abbess. That time expired, the sables were taken down, and preparations made for the inaugura-tion of the new abbess; she approached the altar supported by the elder nuns, followed by the rest of the sisters in procession, who paired off and ranged themselves along the middle aisle. The bishop having read to her the various articles she was bound to observe, explained her duty and administered the oaths usual on the occasion. She was led from the altar to an elevated seat, and the nuns repaired to a gallery appropriated to their use, and a solemn anthem was sung. The ceremony concluded by a hymn, sung by four novices, at that time belonging to the convent.

Constance shone conspicuous among the rest of her competitors for beauty and elegance of person, which even the plainness of her garb did not diminish. Her voice was seraphic, and the skill and judgement with which she executed her part, increased the admira-tion her appearance raised among the spectators. On these occasions, the doors were open to the public, who eagerly seized the opportunity offered. Among the noble persons whom this spectacle had drawn together, was Adolphus, the Count d'Erfeldt. The interesting appearance of Constance riveted his eyes on her, and she was the magnet of attraction, that occupied his thoughts during the solemnity. The day was nearly closed before the ceremony ended. When the abbess and her nuns returned to the interior of the convent, Constance walked with the rest of the novices after the six elder sisters, to whose care they were com-mitted; a murmur of commiseration ran through the spectators at the sight of Constance, who was soon to be lost to a world she seemed born to ornament. It was observed, that she heaved a deep sigh as she entered the gate of the gloomy edifice; various were the conjectures from what source this mark of sorrow sprung, and none was more affected by it than d'Erfeldt. He condescended to make enquiries among the servants, who were employed about the chapel, to what family this lady belonged; some of them either could not or would not give the desired explanation, till meeting with a lay sister more loquacious than the rest, she informed him that Constance was involved in mystery; she had been in the convent but three years, and had at that time entered it late at night, accompanied by the confessor of the convent, Father Francis. She appeared in a forlorn condition, her garments were drenched with rain, her tresses hung loosely on her shoulders, nor had she either cloak or bonnet to shield her from the inclemency of the weather. She seemed nearly insensible to the objects around her, when she was led by Father Francis to the abbess's parlour. Some of the nuns, who were sitting with the abbess, were ordered to withdraw, and the conversation that passed between her, Father Francis, and Constance, did not transpire.

The conference lasted nearly an hour, when the monk retired, and the abbess ordered a chamber to be prepared for the young stranger, who having caught a severe cold attended with a degree of fever, that threatened danger, was confined during several weeks, the abbess attending her with fond solicitude; and from the period of Constance's recovery, she was to her as an indulgent mother. This account induced d'Erfeldt from its singularity to ask further questions, but the answers he received were not of a nature to satisfy the curiosity raised in his breast; the history of Constance, previous to her entering the convent, had doubtless been known to the late abbess; but it had never transpired among the sisterhood. The lay sister spoke highly of Constance; she believed from the tenor of her conduct since she had the pleasure of knowing her, that from whatever source her distress and poverty arose, it was wholly free from guilt, and could only have been from some sudden event, as afflicting as it was unfortunate; for the accomplishments she possessed testified, that her education had been attended to with great care and expense. In general her behaviour evinced frankness of disposition; but she had never been heard to mention her parents, or give the least hint relative to her family, and if any of her companions introduced a conversation that led to such a subject she retired, or if that was not possible, started another theme.

D'Erfeldt retired with a determination of banishing the lovely Constance from his thoughts, but it was not possible, her image was rooted there, and he felt the most ardent desire to be made acquainted with the circumstances that had thus consigned to a convent's gloom the most perfect of her sex. Her expressive countenance was tempered with an innocent sweetness, that led him to coincide in opinion with the good-natured lay sister, that guilt had never been an inmate of her bosom. The situation in which Constance was placed, almost precluded the possibility of seeing her again. He felt interested in her fate, and anxious to know if it was in the power of any earthly being, by pecuniary aid, to ameliorate her woes, and prevail on her to leave the convent; where he supposed (from her countenance, which displayed resignation mixed with melancholy) she had continued more from adverse circumstances, than from inclination. It was an affair in which delicacy forbade his personal interference, nor was it probable that the abbess would condescend, or even deem it prudent to answer the interrogation of a young nobleman with respect to Constance: he made several attempts to get a letter conveyed to the novice, by means of the portress or the gardener, but he was at length obliged to desist, and found they were not to be corrupted from their duty and fidelity. In short he was baffled in every attempt he made to introduce himself to the notice of Constance.

While affairs were in this state, he was suddenly called by an express to attend the Marquis Sperreth, the father of his amiable mother (who had died in consequence of a fright from fire, in one of her accouchements), who was now supposed by his physicians to be at the point of death. The distance was only thirty miles, and the young count, impelled by duty, hastened to the castle of Sperreth with reluctance; at any other time his inclination would have kept pace with the filial respect that he really felt for his relation, from whom, in spite of a ruggedness of disposition he had from his youth, which distinguished him and made him the terror of all who had given him intentional or indeed unintentional offence, he had ever received kindness and liberality.

Though he had not been so fortunate as to gain an interview with Constance, or even to obtain the means of conveying a letter to her hands, yet it was an addition to his misery to be distant from the place that immured her from his sight. On his arrival at the castle, he found that during the preceding night, his grandfather had unexpectedly sunk into a natural sleep, from which the most salutary effects were expected. D'Erfeldt heard this account with pleasure, and he fervently hoped that the returning convalescence of the Marquis would afford him a speedy opportunity of returning to Trent, about two miles from which, situated among the stupendous mountains and terrific rocks, stood the convent of the Grey Penitents. The edifice was only accessible by a craggy path, whose frightful inequalities struck dismay into the breast of a stranger, as it suggested an idea of being at some sudden winding precipitated into a yawning gulph. The Marquis Sperreth continued in a most uncertain state, on one day he appeared to be recovering, and the next he suffered a relapse that threatened almost instantaneous dissolution. Thus did the time pass alternately for several weeks, and Adolphus was in such constant attendance on his grandfather, that he found it impossible, without incurring his displeasure, to make even a temporary visit to Trent. Such was the affection of the marquis for his grandson, that he could scarcely endure a momentary absence, yet in the midst of this endearing cordiality, Adolphus observed something mysterious in the behaviour of his noble relation. At those periods when the excess of his pains made him entertain a belief that his last moments were approaching, he seemed on the point of unburthening his mind of some weighty oppression to Adolphus, and the attendants on his sick chamber had often been dismissed from his presence for that purpose. He would then exhort his grandson to an observance of the injunctions he was about to give him, and not to betray a trust that would devolve to him, when he who was now speaking should be no more. He would in the midst of this address start, and bid Adolphus be careful there were no listeners, and then return to hear the painful truths he had to disclose: then a cessation from pain would alter his resolves and procrastinate the confession to make, which must be humiliating to a man who was in fact proverbial for his pride. He would on these occasions exclaim, "Nothing is impossible while existence is left, and I may yet recover to do justice to those I have injured, and not expose my guilt unnecessarily even to thee! I once thought (continued he), there could be no harm in persecuting the enemies of our faith. I was taught so from my youth, and even that to bring ruin and misery on a heretic was praiseworthy. In the solitude of my chamber I have suffered deeply for this error: conscience has been an avenging judge and an awful monitor. It has taught me that one human being has no right to persecute another for difference of opinions, especially when we both adore one God and Redeemer, and only vary in less essential points."

Such scenes as these frequently occurred, and it was natural for the young count to feel his curiosity excited: that his grandfather had been guilty of some heinous act of injustice, was clearly placed beyond doubt by his self-accusation; this he regarded with surprise. He thought his grandfather possessed of the strictest honour, though neither charitable nor merciful, and quick to punish any act of injustice offered to himself or vassals. He seemed to be indefatigable in discharging obligations contracted by himself to others. Three months had elapsed when the marquis by degrees recovered so far as to be able to sit up for a few hours each evening, while Adolphus strove to amuse him by reading to or conversing with him. One evening his grandfather being in a more cheerful and complacent mood than usual, abruptly put the question to the youth, if he had yet seen the woman whom he supposed capable of forming his happiness in the connubial state. A scarlet suffusion glowed on d'Erfeldt's cheeks, as the image of Constance recurred to his mind. This emotion did not pass unnoticed by the marquis, who observed that he had ever been an advocate for early marriages, from a conviction that they secure persons of both sexes from a variety of excesses and temptations to which human nature is liable, from giving in general a sedateness to the character, which is strengthened by the new and endearing ties that spring up and estrange the mind from frivolous pursuits and degrading connexions. "It is scarcely possible, my dear son (continued the marquis), that I should live to see you in the state I have been extolling; but it would give me pleasure to know that your affections were engaged to an object worthy of an alliance with the noble race of the d'Erfeldts, now represented by you. What says my Adolphus? I know he is candid and sincere." Adolphus was indeed a stranger to every species of dissimulation: he replied, that he had never as yet addressed any lady on serious terms, nor had he till lately seen the woman who could make more than a transient impression on his heart. The conclusion of this sentence led to further explanation, and d'Erfeldt related the adventure he had met with at the convent, and the interest the novice had made on his mind. The marquis at first displayed evident marks of disapprobation, muttering that a novice of such an order could never be a fit bride for his grandson. Adolphus proceeded in repeating what he had been informed of by the lay sister, respecting the fair Constance, and soon perceived the faculties of the marquis to be absorbed in amazement. Three times he made him repeat the account, urging him to be minute in every particular, and on each repetition he burst forth into expressions of surprise. Particularly in questioning him on the length of time that Constance had been said to reside in the convent. He expressed concern and even melted into tears, when Adolphus related the decease of the late Abbess Vitoria Ursula, from a tedious decline. He remarked, it was strange that she had not ordered at least a posthumous letter to be sent him, to announce this awful event.

This remark confirmed Adolphus that his grandfather was no stranger either to the late abbess, or the lovely girl whom she had valued. The astonished youth cast himself on his knees. "Tell me, my lord," said he in supplicating accents, "what is the family and who are the parents of Constance, perhaps you can ease my almost bursting heart, by explaining how she came in her present situation, and what means I can pursue to extricate her from—." Adolphus was at this moment interrupted by a deep groan, and the marquis, overpowered by their late conversation, and the reflections it had given, rose to sink senseless into the arms of his grandson, who conveyed him with difficulty to an adjacent couch, and then alarmed his attendants, who were in an opposite chamber with a physician, who had been retained for some time past in the castle. He was placed in bed and means used to restore him. The emotions that Adolphus had unintentionally given rise to in the breast of the marquis, had been of great disservice to him. He remained dreadfully convulsed during the whole of the night, and such was his situation at the morning's dawn, that the physician declared that it was next to an impossibility for him to survive throughout the whole of the ensuing day. This account was an unwelcome one to Adolphus: he should by this event not only lose a beloved relation, but with him the wished-for intelligence respecting Constance. The physician was indeed right, the marquis expired between the hours of three and four the next afternoon, in the arms of his beloved Adolphus. About two hours previous to this event, he had been able to converse for a short time with the youth; he drew from his bosom a small key, which had hung there suspended by a chain of exquisite workmanship, and presenting it to Adolphus, told him that it belonged to an iron chest, which he had secreted under the altar belonging to the oratory, at the end of the upper gallery, which had been the scene of his morning devotions. "Remember, most dear and duteous boy," said the marquis, "to fulfil the injunctions I am about to give you, as you value my blessings, and wish to prosper. Would to Heaven I had sooner heard what you related last night. I have not time left now to be explicit, the papers you will find in that chest will give you the history of the novice; for the Constance you mention, and the Constance whose loss I mourn, are I am assured the same person; snatch her if possible from a convent's gloom. In that case portion her worthy of my noble house, of which she is a member. My will has been made three years since, with the exception of a few memorials to my friends, and legacies to servants, you are my sole heir, and you are a deserving one. But justice must be rendered Constance, my mind has been poisoned against her by a villain: so long since I have found him, but the discovery was made too late for my peace. From what you relate I am sure Constance was innocent, for she took refuge in the arms of a mother, yes, Adolphus, Ursula was her mother, when I was led to believe her a votary of vice. One-third of my personal wealth I wish to be hers, and such an annuity out of the Vienna estate as you shall think fit, so to your honour and protection I bequeath her. If subsequent events allow of your espousing Constance, remember you have my sanction and fervent blessing, it is an event in which if my spirit could be conscious, it would rejoice. As soon as my remains are deposited in the tomb, examine the contents of the iron chest, and as you deal justly or unjustly by Constance, my blessing or my curse be on you." Adolphus said everything that duty or reason dictated to confirm the marquis in the opinion he had formed of his integrity.

The agonies of death precluded further conversation, except a few short sentences which the marquis uttered at intervals. Above an hour before he breathed his last, his senses forsook him, and he raved about racks, prisons, and convents, in a manner that impressed his hearers with horror. He expired with a groan deep and awful, and Adolphus left the chamber, that he might indulge free from observation the grief he could not suppress. According to the commands of the deceased, his remains lay in state a fortnight, his body being embalmed and screwed down in lead, the room was hung with black velvet, on which was displayed the armour, colours, etc. of the family. The subsequent day to the funeral, Adolphus prepared to follow the commands of the late marquis, with regard to the iron chest. He repaired to the oratory, attended by Gervaise a young man who stood high in his esteem: every vein throbbed with expectation, Adolphus trusting that he should then be acquainted with the mystery that enveloped his fair novice, and instructed in the means to restore her to the world. Bitter was the disappointment that ensued, when on searching the oratory no iron chest was to be found; in vain every part of the castle was strictly investigated, it was still missing. Adolphus was plunged into deep affliction by this unexpected affair: the marquis had been in possession of two other houses, but as he had visited neither of them for ten years past, it was not likely for it to be there. His will, and several papers of consequence were found in safe depositories, but nothing that in the least related to Constance. Adolphus was fearful that her noviciate would be expired previous to his return to Trent, and there was nothing he dreaded so much as being shocked with the intelligence that she was become a professed nun, when the difficulty of obtaining her freedom would be greatly enhanced. He set out to Trent, attended by Gervaise, and they arrived there at a late hour of the evening. He found that his servants, in honour of his arrival and acquisition of fortune, had prepared at their own expense a rural route: tents were placed on the spacious lawn, the groves were hung with coloured lamps, and the festive dance went on among the domestics and tenantry, to the cheering music which was placed at convenient distances among the trees. At any other time Adolphus would have joined with condescension in their festivity; but his spirits were at this time too much harassed to admit of mirth, and he retired to a suite of rooms prepared for his reception.

He felt the utmost gratitude for their intentions, and properly appreciated this mark of their respect; he gave orders for the party to be liberally supplied with every necessary refreshment; a sandwich and some wine was his own supper: he heard the mirth of his dependants with a melancholy pleasure, and sighed to himself, "Ah! how happy should I be, had I Constance for my bride; with what gentle condescension would she treat my humble friends, and share in a certain degree in their respectful mirth." He retired to bed, but his slumbers were disturbed by terrific dreams, the loss of the iron chest was so mysterious and vexatious. Rodolpho and Bernard, the principal attendants on the late marquis, solemnly affirmed that it was in the oratory just before the fatal illness that had caused his dissolution; from the first attack of it, he had never visited the place where it was. They had not the least knowledge of its being removed, nor did they have reason to suppose that anyone, besides themselves and its illustrious owner, knew the place where it was deposited. The next morning, attended by Gervaise, he set out for the convent of Grey Penitents, and delivering in his card to the portress, he soon gained admittance to the grated parlour, where the abbess gave him audience. Her first appearance impressed him with unfavourable ideas: he could not avoid thinking how unfit she seemed to superintend the important trust delivered to her charge; no pious resignation sat upon her brow— no maternal aspect that called forth love and confidence from the nuns was visible—her scowling eyes proclaimed the ambition that filled her soul, and her countenance was not devoid of the traits that mark to a skilful observer the passions of envy and revenge. With a feigned complacence she addressed Adolphus, who was awed by her manner, and at a loss how to commence the business that had brought him to the convent, when he had lost the necessary explanations that the deceased marquis had led him to expect. He stammered out something respecting the commands of the late marquis, with respect to the convent, on the abbess of which he had now the honour to wait. "My revered grandfather," continued he, "had a weight that lay heavy on his mind, alas! he expired without its being removed according to his liberal views, any further than the assurances I gave him of fulfilling his injunctions in that respect: such was his confidence in my honour, he did not admit a doubt of my veracity, and died in a perfect security of his desires being accomplished." Here Adolphus paused—scarcely knowing how to mention Constance, whether by an authoritative demand, or an appeal to the feelings of the abbess: in the latter case he had little hope. The abbess mistaking the cause of his silence, interrupted him with, "Most noble youth, your modest temerity is praiseworthy: allow me, according to my judgement, to relate what I suppose to be the reason of the visit with which I am favoured. The late marquis was, I have every reason to believe, a member that had a laudable zeal for the Church. One of his family, whom he abandoned to her fate for marrying a Protestant officer, at length took shelter within these walls: the marquis, though certainly apprised of the death of his Ursula, means to bestow a handsome gift on our foundation—am I not right, my lord?"

Adolphus beheld the avarice of her principles with disgust: he replied, "A handsome dower shall not be wanting, if I succeed in my purpose. But deceive not yourself, my good lady, no stipulated sum has been left by the marquis; my power in that respect is discretionary, and will be regulated according to the services I shall find the lady Constance to have received from your community, more than in respect to the memory of her mother, whose exemplary conduct, in the station to which the archbishop of B—— elevated her, was an honour to your convent."

"There are doubtless, those," said the Madre, with a countenance inflamed by passion; "as worthy of the trust, as the late Ursula." "It was not my intention to infer aught to the contrary," replied the count; "nor did I suspect, that in praising the virtues of your predecessor I could give you the least offence." The abbess regarding him with a supercilious smile, bade him proceed immediately to the subject that had occasioned his visit, as her time was too precious to be wasted in trifling.

"Briefly, thus," said d'Erfeldt; "you have under your care a novice, named Constance." "Hold, my lord," interrupted the abbess, "nor shock my years by your discourse; Constance is destined to the veil. This is not the first time you have dared to interest persons, whose religious habit ought to have made them sacred from such folly, in behalf of your affection to that artful girl. But to address yourself to me, the superior of the convent, is the height of insolence. Remember, I am not Vitoria Ursula, nor obliged to continue the weak indulgence she showed her favourite."

"Material affection is an excellence in the female character, that I did not expect to hear condemned by one of that sex; and *one* who, by favour of our church, is adopted mother to the number of females committed to her care." "My lord," exclaimed the abbess, "your warmth transports you beyond the bounds of respect due to my character and situation." D'Erfeldt apologised, and the abbess proceeded. "What proof have you to give me, that

Constance is the offspring of my predecessor, an assertion I must own I am not inclined to credit? Let your character for veracity rank ever so high, I am more apt to think, that the violence of your ill-placed passion, has suggested this scheme, from which, however, you are not likely to derive the least benefit. Once more I repeat, what are your proofs?" "There, most holy mother, rests my misfortune: some secret villainy has deprived me of the (to me) invaluable papers, bequeathed me by my grandfather. I have, however, his solemn assurance, that Constance was the daughter of the late abbess; that she had been unjustly persecuted. That it was his pleasure she should be restored to the world, with a fortune worthy of her relations. It is now my present design to demand an interview with that young lady; let it be in your presence. Her account will, no doubt, elucidate those passages that the loss of my grandfather's papers has placed in doubt." The abbess turned from him with disdain, and in a most ironic strain wished him good-morning; and ringing the bell, a lay sister appeared, whom she ordered to conduct the count from the parlour, and see him out of the convent.

When the count returned to the villa at Trent, he gave way to a despair, ill-suited to his youth; the passion he had conceived for the lovely Constance had been heightened by his conversation respecting her with the late marquis; and had affection been entirely out of the question, he would have considered it as an act of justice, to reinstate the fair one in that, to which her affinity to his grandfather entitled her. His painful reflections were interrupted by the unannounced entrance of his friend Baron Steinfort, who had been his chief companion from their infant years.

Perceiving Adolphus reclined on a sofa in a melancholy posture, his dress neglected, and his hair in disorder, he started back, exclaiming, "Gracious heaven! my dear friend, what has happened? I must own I did not expect to find you in full possession of your native vivacity; the death of your grandfather called for a decent expression of grief; but as his decease was neither sudden, nor premature in respect of age, and places you in possession of a noble addition to your paternal inheritance, I cannot perceive the reason of this gust of sorrow." "Frederick," said Adolphus, rising and taking the baron's hand; "I rejoice in your presence, 'tis what I was earnestly wishing for. I should have sent over to the castle, but was informed by Leopold, my steward, that you were at Vienna." The baron explained to him, that he had returned to his castle that morning, wholly unexpected by his domestics, who had not looked for him for some weeks; an affair of consequence having hastened his departure from Vienna. "I heard," continued he, "of your arrival, and having taken a few hours' rest, hastened hither to renew the friendship this long absence has interrupted." Adolphus embraced the baron, telling him, he never, at any moment of his life, had more occasion for a confidential friend, in whose bosom he could pour the sorrows of his heart. The baron made a suitable reply, and Adolphus having given orders to be denied to any company that might call to pay their respects on his return to Trent, sat down to communicate to his friend the vexations he had laboured under with regard to Constance.

The baron listened with attention to the narrative. When Adolphus concluded by asking his advice, he said: "Indeed, d'Erfeldt, from this first step of yours in regard to the wished-for liberation of Constance; I think you have acted decidedly wrong; why make an application to the abbess in this respect? It is not likely she should bear goodwill towards this amiable object; from the very circumstance of her being so high in favour with her predecessor, whose virtues you find she cannot bear to hear repeated. Why not apply to the prince, Bishop of B——, who is now at his palace, not five miles distant from here?" Adolphus observed, that as Constance had not yet taken the veil, he did not think it requisite to apply to such high authority, merely to free her from the temporary vows appertaining to the period of her noviciate. If indeed such an interference was necessary, he had hoped that the abbess would prove his friend, and join in his request; in that hope he was disappointed, and his fears for the happiness of Constance, placed under the power of such a woman, were a heavy addition to the weight of his woes and regret. "Was I," continued the count, "in possession of the particulars of my fair relation, I should know better how to proceed; but I have not the least clue by which to unravel this mystery."

"Forgive me," replied the baron; "in this instance you have been strangely remiss. I wonder that you, who are the lover, should not hit on a point at which to commence your operations; when it instantly struck me on a hearing of your story." "Dearest Frederick,

I am all impatience. How fortunate this interview with such a friend." "Father Francis, the monk who introduced your Constance to the late abbess at the convent, could certainly give you information on a subject, which, from subsequent events, has been rendered so interesting to you. Whether Constance was known to him before that period, or introduced by accident, will then be known, and his mediation in this affair may prove of the utmost service."

"How very dull of apprehension must I have been," said the count, "not to call to mind what you propose. It now strikes me in so obvious a manner, that I wonder how I could overlook it. Father Francis is, if I mistake not, a member of the monastery of St Austin's." "He is so, Adolphus, and I have heard him represented in a most amiable light; mild and intelligent, a *bon* Catholic, but no bigot."

"Just what I would wish to find him," said Adolphus; "we want such a character, to enable us to counteract the malignity of the abbess.—Will you accompany me, Frederick, to St Austin's?" "In this or any other respect you may command me," replied the baron, "and believe me, though I have not the same inducement as yourself to unravel this business, I feel all the eagerness, that friendship for yourself, and pity for an innocent, and I fear injured female, can incite—*se allons mon amie*." The count, with his friend, were chagrined on their arrival at St Austin's, to find that Father Francis was absent on a mission, that would at least detain him for a week; and in the meantime, Eugene, a monk, who had not long received the cowl, officiated at the convent of the Grey Penitents till his return. Mortified at this delay, the count was quitting the portal in silence, but the baron detained him to join in a gift to the porter for his civility; and leaving their cards, desired the reverend man to acquaint Father Francis the moment of his arrival, that they had been there with the wish to consult him on urgent business. The porter having returned them fervent thanks for their liberal donation, assured them he would pay attention to their commands; and the gentlemen returned to the Count d'Erfeldt's residence.

To a youth of d'Erfeldt's temper, this delay was excruciating; all ardour in every affair he engaged with, he could ill brook disappointment: happily for himself and society his propensities were virtuous—guile and seduction he abhorred; had it been otherwise, the talents and accomplishments he possessed might have proved dangerous. A few days after their visit to the monastery of St

Austin's, the veiling of a nun, who was to become one of the Penitents, made a public day at the convent. The count and Steinfort were among the first that availed themselves of this opportunity to visit the chapel. During the ceremony the eyes of Adolphus eagerly sought for Constance; there were three novices attending the abbess, but not the one he sought. A chill ran through his veins, he feared that Constance had taken the veil; perhaps, prematurely forced to that step; for he could not conjecture, by what he had heard from the lay sister, that her noviciate was near the expiration.

He communicated his thoughts to the baron, and they agreed to place themselves by the door that led to the interior of the convent; and Adolphus was to observe the nuns as they passed, with a scrutinising glance, to discover if Constance was of that number. The abbess led the way on their return from the chapel. The nuns and novices passed on in regular order, but there was not among them a form that could have been mistaken, even for a moment, for the lovely Constance. The lay sisters closed the procession. Mary, the humane being from whom Adolphus received his former account of the novice, seemed purposely to linger to the last. She regarded the count with an expression of melancholy. She took a small folded paper from her bosom and slid it into his hand; she then hastened in and closed the door. The count's eagerness to peruse the paper he had received, would not allow him to return to Trent, without making himself master of the contents. He therefore withdrew, accompanied by the baron, to a spot free from observation.

The contents were:

My lord count, in the earnest hopes that I shall have an opportunity of conveying this to your hands, I have ventured to pen these few lines. Constance is yet within our walls; believe not any assertion the abbess may make to the contrary, on your next application for an interview with the amiable girl, which it is reasonable to suppose will not be long delayed. Our Madre is her powerful enemy, from the circumstance of her being the daughter of the late lady Vitoria Ursula, with whom it seems she was formerly acquainted, and who offended, if not injured her. Heaven knows the truth of this assertion: if so, why should the innocent suffer? Be firm in the cause of Constance. Should anything of consequence transpire, I will endeavour to transmit an account to you. Tomorrow, we admit visitors to the chapel; I hope to see you there, when I trust an opportunity will occur to deliver this to you.

MARY

This note was dated on the preceding day, and the visit they had paid to the chapel to witness the ceremony of veiling of the nun (at least, that was the purpose declared, though the real one was the hope to see Constance) had answered to the wishes of their humble friend, the benevolent Mary, who was worthy of a better fate than the veil, to which poverty and early credulity had destined her. The contents of this note heightened their impatience for the return of Father Francis, as they had every reason to dread the power of the abbess.

Much relieved were they when early one morning a short while later, as soon as d'Erfeldt had risen, Father Francis was announced, and invited to breakfast; Adolphus sent for the baron to be present at the interview, introducing him to the monk as his dearest friend and confidant. The first ceremonials passed, the monk entreated to know what particular affair had caused him to be honoured with their commands. Adolphus, in a concise manner, related every circumstance respecting Constance, his deceased grandfather, and the abbess, without betraying the name of the lay sister, from whom he had derived the principal source of his information. He then politely requested Father Francis to relate what he knew respecting the novice. "Most willingly, my lord," said the good monk, "nor have I any impediment to restrain me from a compliance with your request. I had been called out at a late hour one night to attend a dying lady, whose confessor I had long been chosen; as I returned towards St Austin's, I passed the door of a large house near the extremity of the town, it was suddenly opened, and a young female clad in a mourning dress was thrust into the street; she seemed nearly fainting, and would have fallen to the ground, had not I stretched forth my arms to save her. The door instantly closed, and I could hear the bolts drawn across. I was hastening to knock and demand the cause of this cruel proceeding, in exposing a helpless female to the rigours of such an inclement night, and at an hour so improper, but my

purpose was stayed by the entreaties of the young lady, who conjured me, if I possessed humanity, to lead her far from that vile
abode, to some shelter however humble, that might save her from
the insults and dangers she was liable to meet with in the streets.

"I paused (continued the good monk), and recollecting the
virtues of the Madre Vitoria, the abbess of the next convent, I
resolved to take my fair protégée and endeavour to gain her protection within those walls, as it was impossible to give her a shelter
in my own monastery, without risking an unjust scandal; nor would
she be half so comfortable as with those of her own sex. The
abbess was not retired for the night; I sent in a note which I had
scrawled with a pencil, by the light of a lamp, and was soon
ordered into her presence with my charge, at the first sight of
whom the Madre betrayed the strongest emotions. She ordered
the attendant nuns away, and eagerly demanded of the young
stranger her name. 'Constance, daughter of the deceased Count
Kempenfeldt,' was the reply, 'And granddaughter to the Marquis
Sperreth,' rejoined the abbess. 'I am so,' answered the young lady,
with a look that testified surprise at the observation made by the
Madre, who rising from her seat, and approaching her, added to
her astonishment, by opening the collar of her robe, and display-
ing a deep stained mark of a mulberry just above her left shoulder,
to which the abbess glued her lips for a few moments, and then
raising her head affectionately, embraced the weeping Constance,
exclaiming, 'You perceive, my sweet girl, you are not unknown to
me: I have often folded you in these arms; no wonder you do
not recognise my features, they are altered by sickness and sorrow,
nor did you ever behold me in this garb; you are much grown,
but your likeness to your excellent father struck me forcibly the
moment of your entrance. Answer me one question, on which my
peace in a great measure depends; as you hope for heaven's mercy,
swerve not from the truth—I left you under the protection of
your grandfather, you are now a miserable girl imploring shelter
—Has this change been caused by guilt, or misfortune?'

" 'I affirm,' replied Constance, with dignity, 'but that Heaven,
to which I appeal—that I am innocent and virtuous.' 'Then welcome, thrice welcome, to the arms that now enfold you—the arms,
my Constance, of an affectionate mother.' The daughter repeated
the words, 'my mother!' and fainted.

"I feared that my presence was a restraint, and begged leave to retire; the abbess extended her hand, 'Heaven, my good father, will reward you for this deed. Tomorrow we shall be more composed, and you shall hear the story of my Constance; mine you already know; yet it will be necessary to repeat it to my child, and I solicit your presence after vespers.' I was true to the Madre's appointment," continued the monk, "and the abbess and her daughter recounted the events of their life. I will, for the sake of trespassing as little as possible on your time and patience, connect them together. The Marquis of Sperreth was a zealous bigot to the Catholic religion, and detested the members of the reformed doctrine, which was making such rapid strides throughout Germany. Not the books written by, or the discourse he held with enlightened men, who propagated the Protestant faith, could lessen his prejudices against those whom he termed heretics, nor teach him, that charity of opinion was necessary to hold persons of different faith in amicable bonds. He married for his first wife the daughter of a private gentleman, who expired soon after the birth of a female child, who in course of time was married to the Count d'Erfeldt; she bore him several children, but only one survived his infancy; he lost both his parents before he attained his ninth year, and was left to the guardianship of the marquis, who boarded him at the house of an abbé, till he came of age to take possession of his own estate.

"His second wife was the daughter of Baron Holmsbeach, as great a bigot as himself, nor did the fair lady much dissent in principle; yet her manners were mild, and she had no wish to control the opinion of others: not so her wedded lord, for so rigid was his method to force those within his power to an observance of the rites of the Roman Church, that he was apt to inspire terror and disgust instead of admiration. His wife brought him wealth and connection that gave him pleasure; yet she possessed few personal attractions or accomplishments; one daughter was also the only fruit of this union. The mother did not survive her daughter's fifth year, and the marquis was again a widower (in which state he chose to remain), and the lovely Vitoria was left to the sole care of an austere father. She had attained her sixteenth year, when the numerous connections in which the marquis was engaged, through his zeal for defending the ancient religion from more innovations, made his house so much a resort for persons of his own sex, that he did not think it prudent for so young a lady to continue there, as she had no mother to guide her, and her sister being married. He then resided at Vienna, and thought proper to remove her to a château near Tyrol. Her solitude was cheered by the arrival of Josephine, a young lady some years older than herself: she possessed a large fortune, subject to no other control than that, by the will of her father she was obliged to reside under the care of the marquis till her nuptial day; religion had but a slight sway over her mind, and she had long, unknown to Sperreth, encouraged the pretensions of Count Kempenfeldt, a Protestant of engaging manners. Unawed by the presence of the marquis he became a frequent visitor to the ladies, too often so for the peace of Vitoria, who became enamoured with the lover of her friend; she exerted herself to engage his attentions, and at length so far succeeded in her unjust schemes, to flatter herself that, if Josephine was removed, and the count led to believe her faithless, she could attach him to herself. Her plan was arranged, and she lost no time in trying its effects. She wrote to her father a most urgent letter, requesting an interview, desiring at the same time that his visit might appear to Josephine as the effect of chance, and not in consequence of any invitation.

"This letter from Vitoria, and in particular the requests which terminated her epistle, excited his curiosity, and he hastened to the château with the utmost expedition, that he might procure an explanation, which Vitoria was as ready to give as the marquis to receive. She accused Josephine of encouraging the addresses of an heretic, and she stated her suppositions, that if means were not taken to prevent it, a speedy union would take place. The marquis resolved to spare himself that mortification; he asked Josephine to take a morning ride with him, and ere she was the least apprised of his intention, she found herself a prisoner in a convent of the Ursulines, and treated with rigour; to procure her liberty she was obliged to yield her hand to Baron Kanlintz, a husband selected by the marquis, a man old enough to be her father. He was wealthy and the owner of several dwellings; but from some disgust he had taken to the world, he lived in what might be denominated a stately gloom, which was little altered by his marriage. His doors were only opened to a select few, though he retained the same number of domestics as his ancestors had done, when festive mirth and hospitality was the order of the day. But now they were indeed more for show than use. His temper was jealous, and apt to look on the dark side of every object that admitted of a doubt. With such a being it was not likely that Josephine could enjoy happiness. Several hours of each day he was shut up in his study, while the baroness wandered about the fabric like a ghost, or contemplated the stiff portraits of the former inhabitants of the castle. The duty she owed her husband could not always hold its sway over her thoughts, they would revert to Count Kempenfeldt with tears and sighs of regret, as she pictured to herself how much happier the connubial state would have passed with him. She felt an earnest wish to ascertain how he endured their unexpected separation, and whether he had preserved that fidelity fate had not allowed her to maintain.

"She had been married to the baron two months, when her suspense was ended. But the certainty was more excruciating. He was married to the artful Vitoria, a few days preceding the period of this intelligence; it was communicated by the marquis, who in frantic rage deprecated the conduct of his daughter, and renounced her. Absorbed in religious and political controversies, and engaged in his views concerning his ward and her marriage with his friend the baron, he had little time to bestow on his daughter. He indeed wrote to her to know, if he should seek out for some young lady in reduced circumstances, whose accomplishments might render her a desirable companion. Vitoria replied, that solitude was agreeable, that her time was agreeably diversified by her morning walks, and administering to the comfort of the poor peasantry which surrounded her dwelling; reading, working, drawing, and music, had each a share in her occupations, and the young woman who attended on her, being far superior to the usual domestics of that description, she had not one wish ungratified but the desire of seeing her father oftener. This letter gave much satisfaction to the marquis, who delighted to find his child in this frame of mind, and resting secure in the stability of her principles, left her to pursue her favourite avocations. Having removed Josephine, and lulled her father into fancied security, she began her attacks on the count; she made him believe that Josephine's absence was voluntary, and in fact by her own request.

"Disgusted by her supposed perfidy, and the insinuating manners of Vitoria, he soon transferred his affection to the latter, and their courtship was terminated by an elopement, to the chagrin and surprise of the marquis, to whom they transmitted an account of their union with solicitations of pardon, which was refused; a sum of money settled on the daughter by her deceased mother was given to her, with an assurance that was all of her once supposed large fortune she would ever receive, and at the same time intimated, that any future application she might make would not be attended to. The baroness was seized with an indisposition, the consequence of grief, that threatened to terminate her existence, and she continued for months in a pitiable state: the Countess Kempenfeldt heard of her situation, and experienced bitter pangs of remorse, and she was unhappy, though blest with the society of a husband she adored, and for whose sake she had violated the laws of duty and friendship; she wrote to the baroness intreating her pardon and avowing her own repentance, alleging her design to clear Josephine in the opinion of Kempenfeldt, whatever would be the result of such a humiliating confession to herself.

"Whatever consolation the baroness derived from this latter intimation, she would not pronounce the pardon so earnestly solicited, but replied, that her hatred and revenge should always pursue her, and if possible her offspring. Her letter flung the countess into a dangerous state: terror, repentance, and love, were at once too much for her frame. The count was assiduous in his attentions, and earnestly pressed to know the cause of her uneasiness, which she at length unfolded, beseeching Kempenfeldt not to hate her: he listened in silent wonder, and when the countess had concluded, left the room. The manner in which he had lost Josephine affected him; but recollecting that love for himself had caused Vitoria's crime, and the affectionate tenor of her conduct, he resolved on a reconciliation, and to make himself happy with the woman whom fate had ordained his wife, the birth of a daughter added another link to the chain which bound him to Vitoria, and Constance was most fondly beloved by her father. In the fifth year of their marriage the Count and Countess Kempenfeldt were shocked by hearing that the Baroness Kanlintz had eloped from her husband with a young officer to whom he was guardian, and the next intelligence was that the baron, overcome by jealousy, and a high sense of the dishonour his lady had brought upon him, had terminated his existence by poison. They caused strict enquiries to be made after the hapless Josephine, and after some lapse of time they were informed, that stung with remorse for the untimely end to which she had brought the baron, and forsaken by her lover, she had taken refuge in a convent not many leagues from Tyrol.

"The regiment of which Count Kempenfeldt was colonel being ordered on foreign service, his lady attempted to soften the heart of her father, so far that he might receive her and her child under his roof, during the absence of her husband. Vitoria had but faint hopes of succeeding, from the prohibitions formerly received, but it was the will of her lord she should make the attempt, he being loth to leave her exposed to the evils that too often assail a defenceless woman. The marquis consented for her and Constance to become inmates of his dwelling, though he observed that without an express order for that purpose, they were not to intrude themselves into his presence. The count having seen his wife and daughter safe under the roof of the marquis, took a melancholy leave, and joined his regiment. The countess had her own attendants, and an extensive range of apartments appropriated to her use; her commands were obeyed, but she was not admitted to any society with her father, and was even ordered to be careful to avoid meeting him in her walks. She used to behold him from the casements of her apartments, with many a heartfelt sigh. Accident introduced the playful Constance to his notice: the innocence of her aspect, and the replies she made to his questions, took a strong hold on the marquis; and in a few days he felt that existence without her endearing society would be a blank. He hired masters, and spared no pains to render her accomplished. He was a fond parent to Constance; but no entreaties could procure an extension of his kindness to her mother. Count Kempenfeldt died in battle, and his estates being entailed on male heirs, he had little to bequeath his widow Vitoria; in him she lost the only being save her child that could render life desirable. In the midst of this distress she received a letter that added poignantly to her anguish. It came from Josephine, felicitating herself in her rival's misfortunes, which she attributed as a judgement on her falsehood and the miseries she had made her suffer: laying her own crimes and the baron's death to Vitoria's account, as they would never, she said, have happened but for her base dissimulation to the marquis and Kempenfeldt.

"From the marquis she had no consolation, who in fact rejoiced that the count's death had freed his daughter from a heretic. He proposed to the widowed countess to retire into a convent, and by prayer and seclusion expiate the errors of her youth: on this condition he promised to make Constance an heiress to the principal part of his wealth, the other being destined for the young Count d'Erfeldt, the child of a daughter he had by his first marriage. To this Vitoria consented, though the conditions proposed were hard; she was to give up her daughter for ever, never to see or hear from her, and the child was to be taught that her mother was dead. She had no sooner retired to the convent, than she regretted the sacrifice she had made in giving her only child to the implacability of her father; but her promise was past, and it was too late to recant.

"The marquis having thus disposed of the mother, hired a preceptress for the daughter, and a small house was taken for them in a retired situation. He having changed his first design of keeping Constance with him, caprice seemed at this time to have had a powerful effect on his actions; he gave out to the world that his daughter was dead; a mock funeral took place, and a monument was erected to her memory. He seldom saw his grandson, though he loaded him with presents. Adolphus had never heard of the existence of such a being as a granddaughter of the marquis's, as the latter was fearful of their imbibing a passion for each other, that would interfere in his present designs.

"The principal care of Constance devolved on a monk, high in favour with the marquis, though he was wholly unworthy of such a distinction, his life having been marked with enormous crimes. A dissipated nobleman had beheld Constance without knowing to whom she was related: he in vain tried to gain admittance to her residence, for her governess was a woman of honour. The character of the monk was not unknown to him: he applied to him, and met with success. Father Leopold, for a stipulated sum, agreed to place Constance in his power: he did so, and then made out an artful tale to the marquis, describing the girl's absence as voluntary, and that she was the kept mistress of an heretical count. The marquis altered a will he had made in her favour, and forbade her name to be mentioned any more in his presence: telling the monk that the greatest favour he could do him would be to force her into a convent, that she might not add to her disgrace by fresh crimes. Such was the firmness of Constance, that the count found his rhetoric in vain, she answered all his arguments with others that convinced him she would never be a voluntary victim of guilt: while he was meditating the most diabolical schemes, she escaped from his grasp. In vain as the granddaughter of the marquis she entreated shelter; no one gave credit to her story, some treated her as an impostor, and others said, if she was related to that nobleman, he had no doubt renounced her as unworthy of his care; at length she retired to a mean lodging, from whence she made several attempts to clear herself in the opinion of the marquis, by a statement of what had happened. But her letters returned unopened, accompanied by a command from the monk, as he said by the desire of the marquis, that he might be troubled with no more applications. The monk, fearful that he should be discovered in his scheme respecting Constance, and thus lose the favour and rich presents of the marquis, determined to place the fair one in such a situation that would render it impossible for her to seek an interview with the marquis; at the time that Vitoria's death was reported Josephine knew of the deception, and being informed by the monk in what convent the countess had taken shelter, she procured a removal to the same, that she might gratify her revenge and ill-nature, by doing every ill office in her power to the ill-fated Vitoria, who in vain sought a reconciliation. On the decease of the abbess of the Grey Penitents, Vitoria's piety gained her the appointment to that office, to the mortification of her enemy.

"To place Constance under the eye of Josephine was the intention of the monk; he set out to the place where the hapless fair one had taken temporary shelter. He removed her in the dead of the night to the house, at the door of which Father Francis met with her. It seemed inhabited by the vilest of ruffians, and Constance expected assassination; she lay senseless on a miserable mattress, and the monk supposing her to be asleep, talked freely to one of his confidants. The poor girl heard with surprise that Father Leopold was the author of her misfortunes, and also that she was to be removed the next night to a convent, there to be kept in strict confinement, and not allowed to mingle with or be seen by the rest of the inhabitants of the walls. Constance heard this with horror: the monk and his associates withdrew; she was fatigued, but apprehensions kept her awake till the morning's dawn, when she fell, in spite of her efforts to keep awake, into a deep sleep, from which she did not awake till past the meridian of the day. The monk was not there: she found herself under the charge of an old woman and two men of miserable appearance, and found by their discourse that they were subordinate to a set of plunderers. Constance had some jewels on, and her robe was trimmed with rich lace; these wretches agreed to strip her and decamp with the property, as well as some valuable articles that had been left there by the monk and his associates, whose return was not expected till after midnight. The weak resistance of Constance was not of much avail; they forced her to change her dress and its appendages for a miserable black robe, and having completed this scheme, they thrust the poor girl into the street, closely barricading the door, intending to make their own retreat through another outlet. Their villainy, however, proved serviceable to Constance, as she was through this event restored to the arms of a fond mother.

"The monk, on his return to the house, found it abandoned; he was indefatigable in his search after Constance, and by some chance he heard where she was sheltered; as he found that no application was made to the marquis, he suffered Constance to remain in a retreat from whence he thought it was dangerous to attempt to remove her. Since then I have heard that the monk Leopold has been dismissed in disgrace by the marquis, and several of his enormities being discovered, he had fled from the empire with much more wealth than belonged to him. Josephine had interest to procure the succession to the office of abbess, and she was doubtless prompted to this by her knowledge of Constance residing there, that she might pursue the vengeance she had sworn, though she feigned ignorance of such a relationship subsisting. Constance entered on her noviciate at the desire of her mother, as the late abbess would not suffer any application to be made to the marquis, lest her child should be taken from her."

Father Francis concluded this account by advising an application to the Prince Bishop of B——, for an order to liberate Constance, in compliance with the desire of her grandfather. At this period they were interrupted by one of the servants, who informed the count, that there was an aged woman in the hall, who had a letter for his lordship, which she refused to deliver into any other hands, and would take no denial, though repeatedly informed that the count was particularly engaged. The count smiled, and ordered her to be shown into the next apartment, and he would wait on her; she no sooner beheld the count, than falling on her knees she besought him to read her letter, and pardon her penitent son. The count glancing over the contents, saw that they were important; he rang for an attendant, to whom he gave orders for the woman to be supplied with necessary refreshment, and he would see her again. Adolphus read the contents of the letter to the baron and Father Francis. It was from Bernard, one of the attendants of the late marquis. He had, when the iron chest was missing, denied all knowledge of it; a few days back he had been flung from his horse, and now lay at the point of death. He was just able to pen a letter to the count confessing his crime, for which he said his hurt was but a just punishment, for taking a bribe from the lady Josephine to secrete the iron chest the moment his lord should expire, in such a manner that it would be impossible for his heir to discover it; she said it was the intention of Father Leopold to have acted thus, but as he was absent she should trust to Bernard; she added, that it was zeal for the Church that prompted her and not gain, as she could not bear the children of heretics to inherit so much wealth; this last argument ended the scruples of Bernard, and he was true to his promise. His repentance was so sincere, that he entreated his mother to be the bearer of his letter that no mistake might arise, and to implore for him the count's pardon. He described the exact spot where the chest was buried in a vault of the castle. As the distance was but thirty miles, the two noblemen and the monk set out immediately. Bernard died soon after receiving the forgiveness of the count.

The papers contained in the iron chest revealed an awful crime. Count Kempenfeldt did not fall in battle as reported, but was waylaid by bravoes, hired by the marquis to convey him to a place prepared for his confinement; and resisting their attack, was inhumanly murdered. This event embittered the days of the marquis; he could not endure to see his daughter, whom he regarded as the cause of his guilt; he also wished for d'Erfeldt to marry a lady of noble family; he had other views for Constance, and therefore took care to prevent their meeting, fearful of an attachment between them: every domestic was strictly forbade to mention the name of the lady Constance in the presence of Adolphus, who did not know he had such a relation. The young lady to whom he wished to unite his grandson soon after died. Constance had by this time so much engaged his affections, that he resolved to introduce her to Adolphus; when the villainous monk represented her as a disgrace to his name; and he changed his intention, resolving that the knowledge of her being his granddaughter should be carefully concealed from his grandson. The certificates of the marriage of the countess, and the baptism of her daughter, accompanied this explanation.

On their return to Trent, the monk waited on the Prince Bishop of B——, with an account of the transaction, praying that the lady Constance might be liberated from her noviciate; such was the interest this account excited in the breast of the bishop, that the next day he accompanied the Count d'Erfeldt, Baron Steinfort, and Father Francis, to the convent, to demand Constance. The rage of the abbess was easily perceived; she said that the novice, in spite of her vigilance, had escaped from the convent with a young officer. Clara supported this assertion, when sister Mary rushed in, and accused the abbess of secreting Constance in a vault under the castle, where she was perishing with hunger and cold: she also said that sister Clara had the key of this vault. At this discovery the abbess fainted. Having procured the key, they proceeded to the dungeon, where they found the wretched Constance lying on a miserable mattress, praying for death to relieve her sufferings. Adolphus supported her to the parlour. The state of her garments testified the cruelty of the abbess, who, with the vile sister Clara, was degraded to the station of a lay sister, by the bishop: he appointed sister Mary to the dignity of abbess of another society, the rules of the order of Grey Penitents not admitting her to become their superior. Mary chanced to overhear a conversation between the abbess and Clara, which enabled her to save the amiable Constance, who had observed d'Erfeldt in the chapel with favourable sentiments, which had been much enhanced by her conversation with sister Mary, concerning him.——Constance was placed under the protection of the dowager baroness Steinfort, till her marriage with Adolphus took place.

III

CAPTIVE OF THE BANDITTI
A Terrific Tale Concluded

by Dr Nathan Drake and A. N. Other

Bandits also proved popular figures in both the Gothic novels and 'bluebooks'; perhaps their reckless nature and contempt for authority made them seem glamorous characters bringing a little colour into the drab lives of ordinary people. Such men have always been at the heart of 'escapist' literature. It was while I was searching for such a story of banditti that I made one of my earliest discoveries about the ingenuity which it is possible to find in the 'Shilling Shockers'. For in one of S. Fisher's publications simply titled *New Collection of Gothic Stories* (1801), I found the following short story, "Captive of the Banditti". On closer examination it proved to be, in part, a reprint of an uncompleted story by one of the Gothic genre's most notable contributors, Dr Nathan Drake—which had then been 'Concluded By Another Hand'. I read it with fascination to see how the anonymous scribe had finished off the tale of Henry de Montmorency left by his creator at the far-from-tender mercies of some bandits. His plight was a cliff-hanger in the best tradition, and it is interesting to conjecture whether Dr Drake (1766–1836) ever saw the item and whether or not he accepted the conclusion to his story. He had apparently composed it as an exercise in Gothic story-telling, but why he never completed it himself remains a mystery. Aside from his fiction, Dr Drake was an important literary critic and did much to further the cause of Gothic literature, showing particular enthusiasm for Mrs Radcliffe's work. I am pleased to be able to include here the story and its conclusion, I am sure the shade of Dr Drake will not mind sharing this revival of his work with the anonymous 'bluebook' scribe.

THE SULLEN TOLLING of the curfew was heard over the heath, and not a beam of light issued from the dreary villages, the murmuring cotter had extinguished his enlivening embers, and had shrunk in gloomy sadness to repose, when Henry de Montmorency and his two attendants rushed from the castle of A——y.

The night was wild and stormy, and the wind howled in a fearful manner. The moon flashed, as the clouds passed from before her, on the silver armour of Montmorency, whose large and sable plume of feathers streamed threatening in the blast. They hurried rapidly on, and, arriving at the edge of a declivity, descended into a deep glen, the dreadful and savage appearance of which was sufficient to strike terror into the stoutest heart. It was narrow, and the rocks on each side, rising to a prodigious height, hung bellying over their heads; furiously along the bottom of the valley, turbulent and dashing against huge fragments of the rock, ran a dark and swollen torrent, and farther up the glen, down a precipice of near ninety feet, and roaring with tremendous strength, fell, at a single stroke, an awful and immense cascade. From the clefts and chasms of the crag, abrupt and stern the venerable oak threw his broad breadth of shade, and bending his gigantic arms athwart the stream, shed, driven by the wind, a multitude of leaves, while from the summits of the rock was heard the clamour of the falling fragments, that bounding from its rugged side leapt with resistless fury on the vale beneath.

Montmorency and his attendants, intrepid as they were, felt the inquietude of apprehension; they stood for some time in silent astonishment, but their ideas of danger from the conflict of the elements being at length alarming, they determined to proceed; when all instantly became dark, whilst the rushing of the storm, the roaring of the cascade, the shivering of the branches of the trees, and the dashing of the rock, assailed at once their sense of hearing. The moon, however, again darting from a cloud, they rode forward, and, following the course of the torrent, had advanced a considerable way, when the piercing shrieks of a person in distress arrested their speed; they stopped, and listening attentively, heard shrill, melancholy cries repeated, at intervals, up the glen, which, gradually becoming more distant, grew faint, and died away. Montmorency, ever ready to relieve the oppressed, couched his lance, and bidding his followers prepare, was hastening on; but again their progress was impeded by the harrowing and stupendous clash of falling armour, which, reverberating from the various cavities around, seemed here and there, and from every direction, to be echoed with double violence, as if a hundred men in armour had, in succession, fallen down in different parts of the valley. Montmorency, having recovered from the consternation into which this singular noise had thrown him, undauntedly pursued his course, and presently discerned, by the light of the moon, the gleaming of a coat of mail. He immediately made up to the spot, where he found, laid along at the root of an aged oak, whose branches hung darkling over the torrent, a knight wounded and bleeding: his armour was of burnished steel; by his side there lay a falchion, and a sable shield embossed with studs of gold; and, dipping his casque into the stream, he was endeavouring to allay his thirst, but, through weakness from loss of blood, with difficulty he got it to his mouth. Being questioned as to his misfortune, he shook his head, and unable to speak, pointed with his hand down the glen; at the some moment, the shrieks, which had formerly alarmed Montmorency and his attendants, were repeated, apparently at no great distance; and now every mark of horror was depicted on the pale and ghastly features of the dying knight; his black hair, dashed with gore, stood erect, and, stretching forth his hands towards the sound, he seemed struggling for speech, his agony became excessive, and groaning, he dropped dead upon the earth.

The suddenness of this shocking event, the total ignorance of its cause, the uncouth scenery around, and the dismal wailings of distress, which still poured upon the ear with aggravated strength, left room for imagination to unfold its most hideous ideas; yet Montmorency, though astonished, lost not his fortitude and resolution, but determined, following the direction of the sound, to search for the place whence these terrible screams seemed to issue, and recommending his men to unsheath their swords, and maintain a strict guard, cautiously followed the windings of the glen, until, abruptly turning the corner of an out-jutting crag, they perceived two corpses mangled in a frightful manner, and the glimmering of light appeared through some trees that hung depending from a steep and dangerous part of the rock. Approaching a little nearer, the shrieks seemed evidently to proceed from that quarter; upon which, tying their horses to the branches of an oak, they ascended slowly and without any noise towards the light: but what was their amazement, when, by the pale glimpses of the moon, where the eye could penetrate through the intervening foliage, in a vast and yawning cavern, dimly lighted by a lamp suspended from its roof, they beheld half a dozen gigantic figures in ponderous iron armour; their visors were up, and the lamp, faintly gleaming on their features, displayed an unrelenting sternness capable of the most ruthless deeds. One, who had the aspect and the garb of their leader, and who, waving his scimitar, seemed menacing the rest, held on his arm a massy shield, of immense circumference, and which being streaked with recent blood, presented to the eye an object truly terrific. At the back of the cave, and fixed to a brazen ring, stood a female figure, and, as far as the obscurity of the light gave opportunity to judge, of a beautiful and elegant form. From her the shrieks proceeded: she was dressed in white, and struggling violently and in a convulsive manner, appeared to have been driven almost to madness from the conscious horror of her situation. Two of the banditti were high in dispute, fire flashed from their eyes, and their scimitars were half unsheathed, and Montmorency, expecting that, in the fury of their passion, they would cut each other to pieces, waited the event: but, as the authority of their captain soon checked the tumult, he rushed in with his followers, and, hurling his lance, "Villains," he exclaimed, "receive the reward of cruelty." The lance bounded innocuous from the shield of the leader; who turning quickly upon Montmorency, a severe engagement ensued: they smote with prodigious strength, and the valley resounded to the clangour of their steel. Their falchions, unable to sustain the shock, shivered into a thousand pieces; when Montmorency, instantly elevating with both hands his shield, dashed it with resistless force against the head of his antagonist; lifeless he dropped prone upon the ground, and the crash of his armour bellowed through the hollow rock.

In the meantime his attendants, although they had exerted themselves with great bravery, and had already dispatched one of the villains, were, by force of numbers, overpowered, and being bound together, the remainder of the banditti rushed in upon

Montmorency just as he had stretched their commander upon the earth, and obliged him also, notwithstanding the most vigorous efforts of valour, to surrender. The lady who, during the encounter, had fainted away, waked again to fresh scenes of misery, at the moment when these monsters of barbarity were conducting the unfortunate Montmorency and his companions to a dreadful grave. They were led, by a long and intricate passage, amid an immense assemblage of rocks, which, rising between seventy and eighty feet perpendicular, bounded on all sides a circular plain, into which no opening was apparent, but that through which they came. The moon shone bright, and they beheld, in the middle of this plain, a hideous chasm; it seemed near a hundred feet in diameter, and on its brink grew several trees, whose branches, almost meeting in the centre, dropped on its infernal mouth a gloom of settled horror. "Prepare to die", said one of the banditti; "for into that chasm shall ye be thrown: it is of unfathomable depth; and that ye may not be ignorant of the place ye are so soon to visit, we shall gratify your curiosity with a view of it." So saying, two of them seized the wretched Montmorency, and dragging him to the margin of the abyss, tied him to the trunk of a tree, and having treated his associates in the same manner. "Look," cried a banditto with a fiend-like smile, "look and anticipate the pleasures of your journey." Dismay and pale affright shook the cold limbs of Montmorency, and as he leant over the illimitable void, the dew sat in big drops upon his forehead. The moon's rays, streaming in between the branches, shed a dim light, sufficient to disclose a considerable part of the vast profundity, whose depth lay hid; for a subterranean river, bursting with tremendous noise into its womb, occasioned such a mist from the rising spray, as entirely to conceal the dreary gulf beneath. Shuddering on the edge of this accursed pit stood the miserable warrior; his eyes were starting from their sockets, and, as he looked into the dank abyss, his senses, blasted by the view, seemed ready to forsake him. Meantime the banditti, having unbound one of the attendants, prepared to throw him in; he resisted with astonishing strength, shrieking aloud for help, and, just as he had reached the slippery margin, every fibre of his body racked with agonising terror, he flung himself with fury backwards on the ground; fierce and wild convulsions seized his frame, which being soon followed by a state of exhaustion, he was in this condition, unable any longer to resist, hurled into the dreadful chasm; his armour striking upon the rock, there burst a sudden effulgence, and the repetition of the stroke was heard for many minutes as he descended down its rugged side.

No words can describe the horrible emotions which, on the sight of this shocking spectacle, tortured the devoted wretches. The soul of Montmorency sank within him, and, as they unbound his last fellow-sufferer, his eyes shot forth a gleam of vengeful light, and he ground his teeth in silent and unutterable anguish. The inhuman monsters now laid hold of the unhappy man; he gave no opposition, and, though despair sat upon his features, not a shriek, not a groan escaped him: but no sooner had he reached the brink, than making a sudden effort, he liberated an arm, and grasping one of the villains round the waist, sprang headlong with him into the interminable gulf. All was silent—but at length a dreadful plunge was heard, and the sullen deep howled fearfully over its prey. The three remaining banditti stood aghast; they durst not unbind Montmorency, but resolved, as the tree to which he was tied grew near the mouth of the pit, to cut it down, and, by that means, he would fall along with it into the chasm. Montmorency, who, after the example of his attendant, had conceived the hope of avenging himself, now saw all possibility of effecting that design taken away; and as the axe entered the trunk, his anguish became so excessive that he fainted. The villains, observing this, determined, from a malicious prudence, to forbear, as at present he was incapable of feeling the terrors of his situation. They therefore withdrew, and left him to recover at his leisure.

Not many minutes had passed away when, life and sensation returning, the hapless Montmorency awoke to the remembrance of his fate. "Have mercy," he exclaimed, the briny sweat trickling down his pallid features, "O Christ, have mercy": then looking around him, he started at the abyss beneath, and, shrinking from its ghastly brink, pressed close against the tree. In a little time, however, he recovered his perfect recollection, and, perceiving that the banditti had left him, became more composed. His hands, which were bound behind him, he endeavoured to disentangle, and, to his inexpressible joy, after many painful efforts, he succeeded so far as to loosen the cord, and by a little more perseverance, effected his liberty. He then sought around for a place to escape through, but without success; at length, as he was passing on the other side of the chasm, he observed a part of its craggy side, as he thought, illuminated, and, advancing a little nearer, he found that it proceeded from the moon's rays shining through a large cleft of the rock, and at a very considerable depth below the surface. A gleam of hope now broke in upon his despair; and gathering up the ropes which had been used for himself and his associates, he tied them together, and fastening one end to the bole of a tree, and the other to his waist, he determined to descend as far as the illuminated spot. Horrible as was the experiment, he hesitated not a moment in putting it into execution, for, when contrasted with his late fears, the mere hazard of an accident weighed as nothing, and the apprehension that the villains might return before his purpose was secure, accelerated, and gave vigour to his effort. Soon was he suspended in the gloomy abyss, and neither the roaring of the river, nor the dashing of the spray, intimidated his daring spirit, but, having reached the cleft, he crawled within it, then, loosing the cord from off his body, he proceeded onwards, and, at last, with a rapture no description can paint, discerned the appearance of the glen beneath him. He knelt down, and was returning thanks to heaven for his escape, when suddenly——————

*　　*　　*

Concluded by Another Hand

—his attention was attracted by a figure at the entrance of a forest which was on his left hand. Whole shades seemed to declare it a place fitted only for the residence of perturbed spirits, or that of the ferocious and remorseless banditti. It was dressed in white; and in the disordered eye of Montmorency appeared infinitely to surpass the human stature. For a few moments he paused, being transfixed with astonishment at an appearance, which in his present situation he could not help looking on as supernatural.

At length he began to recover from the terror which this new adventure, together with the danger which had threatened him in his former one, had inspired in his breast; when perceiving the mysterious object still before him, he advanced towards it. Forgetting that he was standing on a craggy piece of the rock, he fell to the ground. Stunned with the blow, he lay for some time deprived of sense and motion; and on coming to himself, to his no small surprise, found he was supported by the same figure which had so forcibly engrossed his attention on his first emerging from the horrid chasm, where his unfortunate retinue had met with a fate the most dreadful that barbarity could possibly inflict. The stranger no sooner saw him open his eyes, than she, in the tenderest manner, enquired if he had received any hurt from his fall; to which he answered in the negative; and in his turn demanded who she was, and for what reason she had been induced to wander in that solitary place, and at that mysterious hour (for it was then very near midnight).

The fair fugitive readily complied with his request, and informed him that she was the only daughter of the renowned baron of Dunholm, and heiress to his vast domains. In consequence of which, she had been surrounded by innumerable admirers, and those of the first rank; who all fought for her hand with the greatest avidity. Among these Count Edelbert, a knight of the most profligate manners, found means to ingratiate himself with the baron; who, lured by the ancestry of his family, and the vast domains he pretended to be possessed of, readily accepted his proposals, and commanded Dorothee (for that was the name of the stranger) to look on him as her future husband. This, although her heart was entirely disengaged, and the person of the count was by no means despicable, she could not comply with. A secret horror thrilled through her whole frame whenever her eyes met his. Impressed with these sensations, she ventured to declare her repugnance to the baron. Her father was inflexible, and the day was fixed for her union with the count. A few days previous to that appointed for the approaching nuptials, the count left Dunholm Castle with the utmost precipitation; apologising for his abrupt departure, by saying that a relation of the family, from whom he had also great expectation, had sent for him, as he found his dissolution fast approaching. The appointed moment at length arrived that was to unite the fair Dorothee to the abandoned count, but no Edelbert made his appearance; a circumstance which, at the same time as it created no small surprise in the bosom of the astonished baron, gave infinite pleasure to his afflicted daughter, as she now found her fate retarded a few days longer. In this state of mysterious suspense they remained about a week. Then, one evening, just as the sun had begun to retire behind the western mountains, a special messenger brought a packet for the baron from the Count Edelbert, informing her father that soon after her lover had arrived at the castle of his ancestors, the Danes having made an incursion, and penetrated as far as the castle, had not only spoiled and laid waste that and the whole of his domains, but were also very near taking him prisoner. Prejudiced in his favour, the baron readily gave credence to the contents of this epistle; and was on the point of sending him a consolatory answer, when he received another packet from a friend, who lived in the neighbourhood of the count, informing him that the whole of Edelbert's estates had been seized on, to defray the debts which a life of debauchery and excess had drawn upon him. Enraged at his dissimulation, the baron instantly dispatched one of his vassals with a letter, forbidding him the castle, and informing him that he was thoroughly acquainted with his perfidy. The count appeared much embarrassed on the receipt of this message; but endeavouring to conceal his emotion, he sent the servant back with an answer, that being convinced of the integrity of his own actions, he should leave it to time to clear him from the vile aspersion he laboured under. "From that time," continued Dorothee, "we heard no more of him; and concluded that in order to mend his battered fortunes, he had fled to some distant country; when yester-evening, as my father and myself were returning from Dunholm convent; where, as was our usual custom on an evening, we had been to hear mass, the uncommon fineness of the evening induced us to turn out of the road which led to the castle; when giving the rein to our horses, we were led insensibly to the narrow pass between the mountains; where we had not proceeded many steps before we were attacked by a numerous party of banditti. The baron defended himself with the greatest valour imaginable for a considerable time; when receiving a desperate wound in his side, near his heart, he fell. At that moment the chief of the banditti, in whose ruthless visage I then recognised the features of the profligate count, caused me to quit the horse I rode; and then placing me before him on his own, bore me off to his cavern, in spite of the piercing cries which I uttered, in hopes of bringing some valiant knight to my assistance. Immediately on entering the cavern, I was confined in the manner you saw; in which situation I was doomed to pass my time, until I should consent to become his mistress. From that horrid fate your timely interference preserved me, although you failed in effecting my liberty. I will not attempt to describe my feelings when I saw you overpowered by the banditti. I felt your misfortunes as acutely as my own; and when they led you and your domestics off, to inflict the horrid sentence they had passed on you; unable to bear the horrid ideas which at that moment oppressed me, I fainted a second time. On my recovery, I found the count, who had been only stunned by the blow, his helmet having broken the force thereof, and his vile associates flying up and down the cavern in the greatest confusion, vowing the most exemplary revenge on you; who I now perceived, to my inexpressible joy, had effected your escape in a most miraculous manner. Overwhelmed with fury and disappointment, the banditti at length left the cavern; when finding myself alone, I used every endeavour to obtain my liberty. For some time my exertions proved abortive; but the chain at length breaking, I quitted the cavern and fled on, without once looking behind me, to this very spot, where I have the happiness of meeting with you."

Dorothee finished her narrative, and demanded of her deliverer to return, to what singular circumstance she was indebted for his fortunate arrival. He then informed her that he had left the castle of A——y on the preceding evening during a tremendous storm, accompanied by two of his vassals, in order to relieve and assist such helpless fugitives as chance and misfortune might have exposed to the rude inclemencies of the weather; and then proceeded to inform her of what had passed previous to his attacking the banditti; which was scarcely finished when the ears of Montmorency were assailed by the sound of horses' feet. Raising his eyes, he saw the ferocious Edelbert advancing at the head of the surviving banditti. Driven to desperation, our hero was about to rush into the midst of them, and boldly meet his death; when he discovered another party coming full speed down the opposite side of the glen; whom on their near approach proved, to his no small joy, to be a troop of his own domestics, who had been collected together by one of his former retinue, that had fled in the first engagement. They presented a sword to Montmorency; who having mounted one of the horses, flew to the attack. The conflict was dreadful in the extreme, and for some time victory hung doubtful over the head of either. At length Edelbert falling by the hands of Montmorency, the day was declared in favour of the latter, who having secured the banditti, conducted them, and the lady, to his castle. Thereafter, following the careful burial of the remains of Dorothee's father, and a suitable period of mourning, she became the lawful mistress of A——y Castle by giving her hand to her valiant protector; and together they lived a life of uninterrupted happiness for many years, surrounded by the admiration of all people.

IV

THE SPECTRE MOTHER

Or, the Haunted Tower

Anonymous

Looked at with hindsight, ghosts were undoubtedly the most popular figures from the realms of the supernatural to be found in the 'blue-books'—friendly ghosts, malevolent ghosts; silent, blue-tinged ghosts and racketing, blood-stained ghosts; indeed phantoms of all shapes, sizes and dispositions. In the 'Monk' Lewis School of Gothic horrors the spectre went unexplained: it appeared, passed on its message to the innocent or tormented the evil-doer, and then returned to the spirit world at the successful completion of its mission. Mrs Radcliffe's ghosts, however, usually proved illusionary and were explained in human terms. Nonetheless, both types underlined the appeal of the ghost story, and research through the 'Shilling Shockers' that still exist, and study of the titles of the remainder, clearly show how the appearance of a phantom was universally expected to set the reader's pulse racing. In the light of these facts, I think it is most appropriate to include a typical example here. The item I have selected, however, is interesting for several reasons: first, because it is almost certainly the work of a woman writer and she is also credited on the title page as the author of "Midnight Horrors" and "The Female Pilgrim", two other popular 'Shilling Shockers'. Secondly, because the publisher was a woman, Ann Lemoine of White Rose Court, Coleman Street, in London. In a trade dominated by men, Mrs Lemoine is a notable figure and appears to have been a most industrious lady, publishing three- and four-volume Gothic novels as well as a considerable number of 'bluebooks' on all the popular themes. And just to round off the story, "The Spectre Mother" was also printed by a woman, Ann Kemmish of 17 King Street, Borough.

Records indicate that this Miss Kemmish published under her own imprint as well as producing 'bluebooks' for others.

*   *   *

CHAPTER I

T HE HEAVY CLOCK of Rovido castle had just sounded the last and fearful hour of night; when a man (whose form seemed more than of human stature) stole from the concealment of a dark recess, and with slow and cautious steps, paced towards the more inhabited part of the castle—a long dark cloak shrouded his gigantic figure, and the sable plume of feathers that waved in his hat, shaded a face on which villainy had stamped her pale and terrific image; one hand held a small dark lantern, and the other was raised to his breast, to be assured the murderous weapon it concealed remained in safety.

The assassin frequently paused, for the uninterrupted stillness which pervaded the building, struck to his guilty soul with a sensation infinitely more appalling than the warring of tempestuous elements. He approached a Gothic casement, the sky seemed overspread with one dark cloud, and presented an appearance so gloomy, that even Moresco shuddered as he gazed. Starting from the momentary weakness with which conspiring circumstances had affected his mind, he quickened his pace; and crossing the hall, raised his light to discover the secret door, which led by an indirect way to that part of the building which his dreadful mission called him.

Moresco soon found the object of his search, and ascended a narrow flight of stone steps, leading to a suite of deserted apartments—as he passed through the last of these, he looked cautiously round him, and entered the long and gloomy gallery on which they opened—he stopped to listen—unbroken silence still reigned; and drawing the poignard from his bosom, he gazed on the point, as though to ascertain its sharpness; a convulsive smile distorting his features, as his mind dwelt on the deed he meditated, and its purposed reward.

The murderer proceeded down the gallery, and gaining its extremity, with some difficulty removed one of the marble statues with which it was ornamented; and applying his hand to a panel concealed behind the figure, it yielded without noise, and he entered the antechamber of his intended victims. He replaced the statue, and secured the panel; then approaching a door on the opposite side, bent his ear to the key-hole, and satisfied that all was quiet, he unclosed the door, which led him into a spacious and magnificent bed-chamber. Moresco extinguished the light that burnt in the apartment; and turning his lamp so as to conceal his own figure, with a cautious step he approached the bed, and gently undrew the curtain.

The young and beautiful object of his fatal purpose reclined in the slumber of innocence, unconscious that the poignard of the assassin was, at that moment, aimed at her guiltless life. A lovely babe reposed upon her arm, its sleepless eyes were turned to the features of its devoted mother, and its little fingers playfully entwined in a stray ringlet of her hair. The dark spirit of Moresco shrank from the presence of innocence thus forcibly delineated, and wanted courage to perpetrate a deed so horrible; but at the moment, the mother moved in her sleep, and with instinctive fondness pressed the babe closer to her bosom, as though to save it from the blow that hovered over it—the transient beam of goodness that had broken on the guilty soul of Moresco, vanished before his apprehensions of personal safety, and his thirst for gold; and with a nerved and well-aimed blow, he pierced her virtuous heart, who had never known even a thought injurious to his welfare or his happiness. One faint and quivering sigh alone told the departure of the pure spirit from its mortal habitation.

With trembling eagerness, Moresco drew the bloody weapon from the bosom of the murdered Julia, pointing it (still reeking with the vital current that had so lately warmed the heart of the mother) at the breast of her innocent babe; the infant, unconscious of its danger, smiled in the face of Moresco at the very moment he was about to deprive it of existence, and he paused; the wind arising in a sudden blast, echoed dismally through the chamber, and sounded to the alarmed imagination of Moresco, as a repetition of that appalling sigh, breathed from the lips of his departed victim. He raised his lamp, and gazed fearfully around; the immense size of the room, aided by the dark shade of the hangings and furniture, rendered it impossible for him to discern its extremity by the faint light he bore in his hand; and anxious to hasten from a spot so terrible to his conscience, he snatched the babe from the bed, and had aimed the crimsoned steel, when a vivid blue light flashed on his countenance, and instinctively raised his eyes to ascertain from whence it proceeded, and he beheld the pale shade of the early-fated mother standing before him, her shadowy hand pointing to the corpse, over whose head he traced in characters of blood, and encircled by a lambent flame—"Let the life of the innocent be spared, to plead for the guilty soul of the murderer."

The dagger fell from the powerless hand of the too conscious Moresco, and his whole frame shuddered so convulsively, that he could scarcely support the infant; who, as though infected by the terrors that possessed his mind, clung round his neck for protection. Moresco sank on his knees before the spectre, and pressing one hand to his heart, while the other held the child, without daring to raise his eyes to the phantom, in broken accents articulated a vow to save and protect the infant; and in the next moment, the whole appearance vanished. Soon as his spirits became sufficiently composed, folding the child up in his cloak, he left the chamber; and retracing his steps, quitted the castle without being observed.

Not daring to inform his employer that he had spared the child, he felt the necessity of giving the appearance of its having been destroyed; and consequently taking off its clothes (which were stained with blood), he left them on the banks of a river that was situated within a mile of Rovido; intending to impress the idea of its having been murdered, and the body thrown into the water. He was aware, that it might seem strange, that the child should be destroyed there, instead of in the fatal chamber; but he trusted that its death would nevertheless obtain belief. Having performed this task, and carefully covering the now slumbering child with part of his own garments, he proceeded, and some time before daybreak reached the dreary and retired spot, which, for many months, had been his home.

The well-known rap of Moresco was answered by an enquiry of who sought admittance; and his voice confirming the signal, he was admitted to the lonely habitation.

"Angela!" said Moresco, addressing his wife, "take this infant, and cherish it as thine own: the manner in which we live, since we hold no intercourse with anyone, will make the task of deception easy; and be mindful, as you value the life of your husband, that you keep the secret."

"But may I not know whom the secret babe belongs to?" timidly enquired Angela, "who is its mother?"—"No!" thundered Moresco, "dare again to ring the name of mother in my ear, and thou mayest shudder for thy temerity."—"It is enough, spare this violence, I am satisfied," said the trembling Angela.

"Forgive me," said Moresco in a softer tone, "and if my peace and life is dear to you, swear by the most solemn protestations, never to let it appear that this is not our child; for no one as yet (if you have obeyed me in confining yourself to the seclusion I prescribed you) knows whether we are childless or not; and mark me, should any observation be made on the sudden appearance of the infant, the tale must be, that I have fetched it from a relation afar off, no matter where."—"I have in every thing obeyed you," replied the meek Angela, "and still promise to fulfil your commands."

" 'Tis enough," said Moresco smiling horribly, "we will think no more of it: bring me some spirits, for I would teach my soul forgetfulness of—of—and drink thy health, Angela," he added, rubbing his hand over his forehead, as though to collect his confused ideas.—Moresco filled a small goblet with brandy, which he eagerly swallowed, and replenishing the empty vessel, turned towards the fire, and stirred it into a vivid blaze.

"What a melancholy stillness has pervaded the air tonight," said Angela, looking timidly around her; "methinks it has impressed my fancy with a more than usual terror of this gloomy tower; for I seemed to hear—" "What?" eagerly demanded Moresco. "Nothing," replied his wife, terrified at the severity of his manner, " 'twas but the conjuring of a disturbed imagination." "I would know the idle fancy that disturbed thee," said Moresco, "I pray thee, tell it to me." "As near as I can judge," replied Angela, "it was about half an hour past midnight, when, sitting on the chair which you now occupy, I heard"—"What did you hear?" hastily interrupted Moresco. "At half an hour past midnight!" he added in a muttering tone.—"Yes, my lord," replied Angela, "it was at that time. I sat meditating on what could have so long detained you; when, on a sudden, both my lamp and fire burnt with such dimness, that I could scarcely discern the furniture that was near, and a sigh so soft, and yet so dismal, sounded on my ear, that it sunk on my heart with a sensation of extreme terror."

Moresco struck his hand on his forehead, his whole frame trembling with the agitation of his mind. Angela was terrified at the emotion he betrayed, and felt an apprehension and horror, to which she could assign no name. "We will to rest!" said Moresco, rising from his seat, and emptying the flask that stood before him. "Methinks you have infected me with these fancies; another time, and I will laugh thee out of them, but now I would sleep," he added.

Angela lit a taper, and in silence preceding her husband, entered their chamber. Moresco approached the bed, but his eyes resting on the babe who reposed in quietness upon it, he shrunk back. "Why do you start so?" asked Angela, observing his agitation. "Saw you nothing?" demanded Moresco, looking wildly at her.—"No, my lord, nothing; do not gaze so fearfully; you terrify me: I pray you retire to bed."—"I cannot sleep by that child," said Moresco; "take it away."—"Let it remain tonight," returned Angela, "there is no other couch prepared." "Well, be it so; tomorrow, you must provide for it": and recollecting himself, fearful of more alarming the mind of Angela, he conquered his repugnance, and went to bed.

The mystery that attended the child, Moresco's seeming horror on beholding it, and the extreme agitation of his mind, were subjects too harassing to the feelings of Angela to allow her to sleep; and pressing the babe in her arms, who had instinctively crept towards her, she mused with terror and curiosity on the incidents of the night; from the contemplation of these images, her distressed mind wandered to a no less painful, though a far different subject of meditation. She dwelt on the vicissitudes of her own destiny, and tears fast flowed down her cheeks as her fond heart throbbed with tender recollections of the friends who had cherished her infancy, and the lover, whose faithful affection had blest her maturer youth; the first had long slumbered in the grave, but di Montmorenci might yet exist, though not for her: the unfortunate Angela might never again listen to the soothings of his voice, or dwell again in reality on that countenance, memory delighted to recall.

CHAPTER II

ANGELA MODENI was the daughter of humble, though respectable parents, left an orphan and destitute at an early age; the Marchioness di Montmorenci (a Venetian lady, who had known and esteemed the Signora Modeni) took her under her protection, and bestowed on her an education that rendered her a suitable companion for her patroness. Happy in the kindness and affection of the marchioness, she reached her twentieth year; at this time, the young Marquis di Montmorenci returned from abroad, whither he had spent the last three years; Angela had seen him before, but for so short a period, that the charms of his mind and disposition had not had sufficient opportunity to display themselves; but now that Venice had become his residence, she could not long remain blind or insensible to the singular merit and interest of his character. Alarmed at the growth of an attachment she could not hope would terminate happily, she sought to avoid the society she loved. Di Montmorenci felt in his own heart sensations that immediately explained the conduct of Angela, and his love kept pace with the esteem the virtue of that conduct excited.

The marquis, despising the advantages of rank, when placed in competition with worth and happiness, declared his affection to its fair object; and, in defiance of the resolution of Angela to conceal its reciprocity, drew from her the acknowledgement he wished; but though he had so far succeeded, no entreaties could induce her to forget the debt of gratitude and duty she had incurred towards her benefactress; and she steadily refused to comply with the pleadings of affection, since she could not hope to obtain the sanction of the marchioness, who depended on seeing her son form an alliance of equal birth. Yet, though she felt assured, she would never be the wife of di Montmorenci, there was something so soothing to the mind of Angela, in the certainty of being beloved where she was herself so strongly attached, that her own affection rather increased than diminished; perhaps, the consciousness of having made a sacrifice to virtue of its dearest wishes, acts as a stimulus to a pure and exalted love; at least, it seemed so in Angela, for, from the moment she relinquished her lover, the sentiment became imbued with every feeling and every thought of her soul.

Di Montmorenci, less capable of bearing the disappointment, soon discovered to the quick eye of the marchioness the secret that corroded his heart, and inexpressibly alarmed for the happiness and future establishment of her son, she immediately determined to remove Angela from his society. The marchioness was at a loss to conjecture whether his affection was returned, and judging it best for her own views to suppose it was not, since she could not well dispose of Angela without assigning some motive, she determined to impart to her, her suspicion of the cause of di Montmorenci's evident uneasiness; and by appealing to her gratitude and affection, to induce her to retire without his knowledge for some time to a distant convent, the name of which was to be kept concealed.

The attempt succeeded to the entire satisfaction of the marchioness. Angela, struggling to conceal the tenderness of her own heart, consented; and everything being arranged, she left the castle a few mornings afterwards before daybreak, accompanied by a male and female domestic—the lady di Montmorenci, intending to acquaint her son in the course of the day of her motive, and the steps she had taken.

Meantime, Angela, with a heavy heart, proceeded on her journey; towards the conclusion of the second day, they entered on a large and gloomy forest, night closed around them, and the sound of a banditti's horn echoed amidst the trees; in a short time, the travellers were surrounded, and Angela and her attendants taken prisoners to the caverns they inhabited. The loveliness of Angela's person attracted the attention of Ludorico, the chief bandit, and he ordered that every attention should be paid her; Moresco, the second in command, surmised the motive of his captain's urbanity, and equally charmed himself, determined to defeat his purpose.

Moresco was the youngest son of a Neapolitan nobleman, from whom he had inherited an estate; incapable of supporting the claim of his extravagant and dissipated conduct, he endeavoured by gaming to retrieve what he had lost, but in the attempt, deprived himself of the small portion which remained: grown desperate from the ruin that involved him, he had recourse to fraud and artifice to support himself; and at length being detected in one of his dishonourable actions, a duel ensued, in which he killed his adversary. Obliged to leave Naples, he met on his journey a party of Ludorico's men, and was conveyed to their chief, by whom he was soon persuaded to join the association; and distinguishing himself in many enterprises, he ascended step by step, till he became second in command.

Desirous of avenging himself against Ludorico, who had openly disapproved his conduct in a late expedition, he resolved at once to disappoint the wishes of his chief, and secure the person of Angela for himself. For this purpose, he warned his intended victim of her danger with regard to Ludorico; and urging her, by the most plausible entreaties, arguments, and protestations, to depend upon him to save her from the fate her own prior observations had taught her to dread, she confided in his honour, and suffered him to remove her from the cave. He protested, that had it been in his power, her female attendant should have been the companion of her flight; but this (he added) was useless to attempt. Fearful of trusting to Moresco, yet still more terrified at remaining with Ludorico, Angela was obliged to make choice of the evil that appeared the lightest, and trusting in heaven, that all its decrees (whether happy or afflicting in their present appearance) tended towards some wise and good purpose, she accepted the protection of Moresco to lead her from captivity.

Her companion was not long in revealing the reality of his motives and intention; and the unhappy Angela found that she must either consent to unite her fate to his, or submit to an alternative she should not fail to reject.

Moresco had really imbibed a passion that made him desirous of entirely securing its object, and believing that such a mind as Angela's would consider a consecrated vow binding, however repugnant to her feelings; and that he should, by allowing her a choice, make himself appear in a light somewhat more deserving of her favour, he offered her marriage. Despairing of succour, she was obliged to comply; and Moresco procured a priest, whom the power of gold easily influenced to perform the ceremony; and the nearly insensible Angela, scarcely able to articulate what was requested of her, was borne in triumph from the altar by the unprincipled Moresco. Fearful of the consequences to himself, should he be discovered, he removed to a considerable distance from the haunts of the banditti; and assuming a different name to that he had borne while with them, he fixed his residence in one of the most desolate parts of Italy, in a deserted and ruined tower. This habitation well suited the purpose of Moresco; for the many and fearful tales that were related of it, secured him from the danger of intrusion on his solitude, and he had strictly enjoined Angela to abstain from any intercourse whatever.

The next care of Moresco was to provide for the support of himself and wife; and this he effected by private depredations at night, in the environs of a town, situated a few leagues distant: in one of these excursions, chance introduced him to the Count Ruvello, who soon understanding his character, gave him a mission, which promised him too large a reward to be withstood. The husband of the ill-fated Julia had lately fallen in the field of warfare; and by his will, he decreed his immense possessions to his wife and child; but in case of the decease of the mother and the daughter unmarried, the whole of his fortune was to revert to his kinsman, Count Ruvello. This intelligence no sooner reached the ears of the count, than he felt a restlessness and inquietude that continually tormented him, and by degrees, the horrible idea of murder stole into his mind; and Moresco was fixed on, and agreed to perpetrate the deed—how he performed that agreement is already known.

CHAPTER III

M O R E S C O, soon as it was daybreak, awoke from an uneasy sleep, and immediately equipped himself in the garb of a friar (telling Angela he should not return till two days after the ensuing), and set out for the dwelling of Count Ruvello; it was night before he reached the palace of the count, and being informed he had retired, oppressed with the mournful intelligence of his kinsman's death, he, with seeming devotion, crossed himself.

"Perhaps, holy father," said the porter, "my lord may find comfort in your pious consolation; tarry a moment here, I will communicate thy wish to see him." The man shortly returned, and desiring Moresco to follow him, ushered him into the antechamber of the count.

Ruvello, as his eye rested on the gigantic figure and stern visage of Moresco, retreated a few paces from him; the varied hue of his countenance, imparting the feelings of his mind.—"Why do you shrink from me, my lord?" asked the assassin contemptuously, "do you repent?"—"Repent!" said the count in the same tone, "no, signor, methinks my courage is scarcely less dauntless than thine; but this is idle, hast thou done the deed?"—"I have!" replied Moresco. "But wherefore," demanded Ruvello, "didst thou destroy the child out of the castle?"—"Because," said Moresco, "as I was about to stab it—but, hark! what was that? was it you, my lord?" he asked in accents of terror.—"Me!—what?" demanded Ruvello, even more alarmed. "Did you not sigh, my lord, just as I spoke of the child?"—"In truth, I know not," said Ruvello; "but it is possible—I have a habit of it." "Well, my lord, to be brief," rejoined Moresco, speaking hastily; "just at the moment that I would have destroyed it, a sudden noise in the extremity of the chamber alarmed me; and in the first impulse, I retreated with the child in my arms, and making towards the river, I took from it its clothes, fearing they might entangle with something so as to save its life, and plunged it into the water."

" 'Tis well, signor," replied Ruvello, "thou hast done the business to my satisfaction, and wilt find the promised sum in this bag; but, for the sake of appearances, you will, as before agreed upon, remain a day or two in my palace, under the semblance of soothing my mind in its affliction." Moresco bowed, and the count intimating to his servant, his wish of retaining the friar for some short period, apartments were prepared for his reception.

CHAPTER IV

A N G E L A, unable to sleep, arose soon after the departure of Moresco, and kindling a fire in the chamber, sought to enliven by its blaze the dreariness of a November morning. Though the society of the man, circumstances had compelled her to marry, could never be otherwise than repugnant to her feelings; yet the prospect of spending so many hours alone, in the gloomy ruin they inhabited, cast a painful depression on her spirits. She endeavoured to find in the cherub smiles and sportive fondness of the babe towards its new protector, a relief from the heaviness that oppressed her; but there were ideas of such painful incertitude connected with every thought of the child, that it rather added to, than relieved the weight she endeavoured to lighten. At length the weary day closed, and the heavy clouds that had obscured the sun, seemed gathering together, intimating an approaching storm. Angela had early put the babe to rest; but a terror for which she could scarcely account, so impressed her mind, that sleep seemed banished from her eyes; and she continued to sit by the fire in her chamber.

'Twas now past midnight, and the storm that had been long threatening, burst over the ruin with sudden violence. Angela started from her seat, and gazed with horror around her; the vivid lightning that flashed almost incessantly through the casement, revealed with terrible effect the awful sublimity of the scene without.

Angela turned, shuddering from the view, and scarcely daring to either breathe or raise her eyes, approached the bed, believing, that even to be near the infant would cheer the dismal solitude of all around; but scarcely had she gained that part of the chamber in which the little innocent reposed, than a sudden effulgence burst upon her sight, and a pallid and bleeding form, encircled by a pale blue vapour, stood before her. Angela, petrified to the spot, stood gazing in wild amaze upon the awful being, as it slowly glided before her; it reached the bed, and the curtains, as influenced by a supernatural cause unclosed—and the phantom, with a look of the most mournful tenderness, bent over the slumbering babe; then turning towards the still motionless Angela, with one hand raised towards heaven, and the other pointing to the wound, it motioned her to follow. Angela, not daring to obey, still remained in the same attitude; the object she dreaded, and yet revered, looked beseechingly at her, and by the most impressive and solemn manner, silently implored her compliance: by degrees, the terrors that pervaded the mind of Angela subsided, a pious enthusiasm elevated her feelings, and revived her courage, and believing that she was selected as the humble agent of some important event, she resolved to obey and comply with the silent direction of the spirit, to take the slumbering babe in her arms; with trembling and slow steps she followed. As the spectre reached the extremity of the apartment, a concealed door flew open, and the startled Angela perceived a narrow and dark passage, the length of which her eye could not discover—the phantom glided through the aperture, and in awful silence proceeded—a pale stream of supernatural light revealing the part of the building they were thus traversing. The passage they had entered, wound for a considerable way—at length the spectre paused, and raising both her arms upwards, looked impressively at Angela; a sigh, such as she had heard on the night preceding, now burst on her ear, and ere her harrowed senses had recovered the shock it gave them, the phantom sunk in a moment from her sight: and in place of the spot on which it had stood, she beheld a dark and apparently immeasurable chasm.

Angela, with sudden and resistless force, felt impelled to descend the half-ruined steps, leading through the dreadful abyss; many times she paused ere she gained the bottom to ascertain its depth, but in vain, so faint was the light, and so black the gloomy vault in which it ended. Shuddering with terror and dismay, on finding herself in a place of such silent horror, she wanted courage to look towards the immense height from which she had descended; but a low rumbling sound breaking over her head, in a moment urged her to raise her eyes, and with horror too poignant for description, she beheld the chasm closing over her, so as to preclude the possibility of her return. Scarcely able to support the child, she leaned against the damp wall of the dungeon—her blood seemed congealed in her veins, and her nerveless limbs shook with convulsive motion.

For several minutes Angela had remained in this situation, when her name, thrice pronounced in solemn sepulchral accents, broke on the profound stillness that pervaded the spot; and the shadowy hands of several scarcely visible forms gliding through a thick and dusky vapour, beckoned her forward. With desperate courage, she obeyed the mystic summons and proceeding through a long range of subterraneous chambers, at length found herself at the entrance of a vault of an immense size and irregular form; as she passed into this dreary receptacle (for she found that it had served the purpose of a common sepulchre), her supernatural guides became gradually more indistinct, and soon entirely faded from her view. Angela perceived a ray of light beaming through this melancholy spot, but a projection of a wall, which had been designed as a partition, prevented her discovering whence it arose; urged by the mixed sensations of hope and fear, she advanced towards it, and turning the half-ruined partition, her eager eyes rested on a scene that seemed to transfix their gaze.

The phantom that had urged her visit to this abode of horror, stood by an altar of black marble, on which the flame of a lamp cast an imperfect and melancholy light; large spots of crimson blood stained the sable stone, and fragments of human bones lay strewn upon the ground. The phantom motioned Angela to approach, and with desperate resolution, she obeyed the summons; as she reached the altar, the death-cold hand of the spectre pointed to a small recess in the marble; Angela, comprehending the meaning, bent her eye to the spot, and observing that it concealed something of uncertain form, she drew it forward, and in a moment discovered it to be a dagger steeped to the hilt in blood. A more ghastly and livid hue diffused itself over the deathly features of the spectre, still pointing one hand to her bosom, with the other she directed the eye of Angela to the fatal weapon, who, with horror too strong for language, traced the name of Moresco carved rudely on the hilt.

"Angela! Angela!" pronounced the spectre in solemn accents, "thou art called upon to save the innocent from the snares of the guilty; bear her, even this instant, from the power of her mother's murderer. It is the Count Ruvello authorised the deed, and thou must restore to her the inheritance he has usurped. Fear not to act with firmness, thy virtue shall produce thy happiness."

A sudden stupor pressed on the senses of Angela, and without being conscious of the means by which she had been conducted, she found herself, on reviving, in the open air; and looking round, saw that she reclined on a small bank, a few paces distant from her house. Every incident of the last two hours was fresh in her memory; and animated by the awful solemnity of the whole, she resolved to obey the sacred injunction of her midnight visitor; and gazing on the child, which still slumbered in her arms, with a mother's interest and fondness, she proceeded down the road, to which she had been unconsciously conducted.

The storm had ceased to rage, but the black clouds still hovered in the air, bespeaking a renewal of its violence. Angela exerted herself to the utmost, and had pursued the path for more than a league, when the rain began again to descend, and faint flashes of lightning crossed her path; she redoubled her speed, and discovering a large building at a short distance, she hastened towards it, trusting its inhabitants would afford a temporary shelter for herself, and her precious charge.

The drawbridge was down, and Angela entering the courtyard, crossed to the grand door or entrance, and raised the bugle to her lips, but her faint breath was insufficient to produce a sound by which she might hope to be heard, and after many successless efforts, she left the spot, trusting to find a postern, through which she might gain admittance. Angela was not deceived in this expectation; at a short distance from the principal door, she found a smaller one half unclosed, through which she passed into a passage; here she would have remained (fearing to proceed), but the current of air was so strong, that she had too powerful apprehensions for the comfort and health of the child, to allow her to continue; and cautiously proceeding to the end (for it was still too dark to see her way), she found herself at the foot of a staircase. Angela ascended the first flight, and feeling that there was yet another, she determined to go no further; but seating herself on the bottom of the second, she wrapped the infant in the foldings of her robe, determined to await there till daybreak.

An hour elapsed, and the harassed fugitive, wearied by the fatigue and agitation she had suffered, had nearly fallen asleep, when the sound of a slow step upon the stairs, roused her from the momentary forgetfulness that had stolen over her, and hastily rising, she endeavoured, without noise, to ascend the remainder of the steps; but for want of light to guide her, she had nearly fallen over a loose fragment of stone that had been dislodged from the wall, and the shock it occasioned awakened the child, who immediately began to cry.

The person who was behind quickened his pace, and Angela, who had now gained the top, with one hand extended, to observe if anything impeded her progress, ran down a long gallery; unable to proceed further, and hearing no sound of pursuit, she seated herself on the floor, and gently laid the babe, who was now quiet, in her lap; endeavouring, by rubbing her hands and temples, to dissipate the faintness that every instant increased upon her; but the effort was vain, and in a few moments she sank to the ground wholly insensible.

The child, who was still awake, stole from her lap, and creeping on its hands and knees to some little distance, renewed its cries; the sound directed the man who had before heard it to the spot; though still in the dark, he found the child without discovering the unconscious Angela; and taking the little innocent in his arms, he left the gallery in order to relight his taper, which a draught of air had extinguished on his way back to that part of the building which he inhabited, intending to return to look for the man, or woman, whom he supposed had dropped the child. Angela, before this could be effected, had recovered; and missing the infant whom she fruitlessly endeavoured to find in the gallery, resolved to hazard every consideration of self to secure its safety. In a state of mind bordering on frenzy, she entered a suite of apartments leading from the gallery, which in vain she searched for the treasure she had lost; at length the reflection of a lamp shining through a half-opened door, struck on her gladdened sight, and she eagerly rushed forward, believing, though a savage should inhabit it, he could not refuse her the boon of a taper and assistance in her anxious pursuit; but what could equal her joy when, on entering the chamber, she beheld the sweet object of her distress reclining on the couch, on which the blaze of a good fire shed an enlivening glow; she sprung towards it, and the babe, as though it knew her, smiled through its tears, and stretched out its little hands to meet her embrace. Angela folded it to her bosom, and her agitated spirits relieved themselves in tears.

Ere Angela has ceased to weep on the bosom of the child, the being whom she dreaded, entered the chamber, and fearful of raising her eyes to a countenance, in which she might possibly trace a character of villainy, she remained trembling, and kneeling by the couch.

"Fear not, lady!" said a voice, that every nerve acknowledged. —She could not answer; she could not speak; but almost convulsed with dread and expectation, she started from the couch, and in the next moment, sank in the faithful bosom of di Montmorenci. Many, many minutes elapsed, before the impassioned exclamations of di Montmorenci recalled the fleeting senses of the beloved Angela; though scarcely able to support the idolised being he held to his bosom, the lover had not resolution to resign, in a moment of such happiness, the treasure he had so long and fruitlessly sought; and when Angela revived, she unclosed her eyes on the dearest object that had ever greeted their sight, and felt the warm beat of that heart, whose affection had entailed on her so much happiness, and so much of misery. Beloved Angela!—Ever-remembered di Montmorenci! was all that for some time they could articulate, till Angela withdrew the arm, that, with the instinct of affection, had encircled the neck of her lover; the action presented both to her own and his eyes, the fatal token on her finger, that told him his hopes were blasted, and reminded her of her duty to another.

"Angela! Angela!" exclaimed di Montmorenci, impetuously grasping her hand. She understood the question, and with faltering accents confirmed the dreaded information. Di Montmorenci burst from her, and throwing himself on the floor, endeavoured to stifle the agony that unnerved his mind. Angela approached him, and alarmed by the violence of his affliction, endeavoured to soothe him; her voice, her language, was too powerful to be withstood; and though he felt the fatal wound he had received, sink every moment deeper into his soul, yet the violence of his emotions decreased, and he listened with as much calmness as it was possible for a lover to do (who was so ardent and so devoted) to the painful narrative of the unfortunate Angela. As she came to that part of her history where the child was committed to her care, she hesitated to proceed; she knew that she could not accuse Ruvello without endangering the life of Moresco, and this, though resolved never again to see him, she would not determine upon; yet in what way could she fulfil the mission that heaven seemed to have entrusted to her, without bringing to light the villainy of the count. And surely the welfare of an injured innocent, so solemnly given to her care, ought to supersede every other consideration. But to reveal to di Montmorenci these circumstances, was to ensure certain punishment to Moresco, should Ruvello confess him an accomplice; therefore, after much mental deliberation, she imparted her wish to the marquis to confer with some holy monk on a subject of much importance; and for herself, that she should wish, if practicable, to remove with the child to a convent, in the morning, for at least some time.

"There is a pious father, resides in the monastery near this ruin," returned di Montmorenci; "in the chapel belonging to this castle is deposited the remains of his beloved brother; and on the night in which I sought rest within its walls, he was visiting the tomb; chance directed me to the same spot, the sympathy of sorrow drew us towards each other, and we mutually revealed our griefs. The good man saw that I was weary from exertion, and would not suffer me to quit this place, till he should give me permission: he has spent much of his time with me, endeavouring to soothe my broken spirit, and to urge me from a pursuit he was convinced was useless in itself, and highly injurious to my health and peace of mind. Gratitude for his kind intent, and the consolation I derived from his pious precepts, urged me from the present to comply; and never can I be sufficiently thankful (added di Montmorenci, raising his fine eyes to heaven) for a detention so providential in the event."

At the request of Angela, he now related all that had occurred since they last parted; with cautious tenderness, he broke to her the death of his mother, and then proceeded to recount the many different methods he had pursued, and the journey he had himself undertaken, attended only by one faithful domestic, to discover the fate of the beloved Angela; for the female who had suffered imprisonment with herself, had afterwards escaped, bringing intelligence of Angela's migration from the cavern in the company of Moresco, who had been known to the robbers by a different name.

Di Montmorenci had scarcely ceased speaking, before his attendant announced to him the approach of Father Bernada; the good man soon after entered the room, and with a heart-felt delight, welcomed Angela, to whom di Montmorenci introduced him. Anxious to make the communication she meditated, she requested an audience of the monk, and di Montmorenci leaving the room, she made an undisguised confession of all that had occurred; the father listened to her with astonishment and awe, and urging the necessity of bringing the Count Ruvello to justice, as a duty not only of moral obligation, but enjoined by heaven, promised to take its management upon himself; at the same time acceding to the wish of Angela, should the count forbear to implicate his confederate, that the guilt of Moresco should be screened, unless absolutely necessary to reveal it. Relieved from the burden that oppressed her, she gratefully thanked the good man for his advice and services, and gladly accepted his recommendation to a convent in the neighbourhood, whither, on leaving her, he immediately went to secure her a reception.

Di Montmorenci, satisfied by the assurances of the monk, that the confession of Angela revealed no error of himself, endeavoured to calm his mind under the heavy disappointment it had suffered, by the assurances of her unalterable friendship; and by the consciousness, that if not raised to happiness, she was at least removed from misery. In the course of the morning, Angela, with the little orphan, repaired to the convent; whither she bade the sad di Montmorenci not to seek admission to her, until they had both learnt to meet without a painful regret obtruding on their minds. Di Montmorenci promised with a sigh, that seemed to express, if he must cease to love her, they would never meet again.

The lady, mother of Santa Maria, received her guests (of whose story she had heard sufficient to deeply interest her) with true kindness; and long unused to society of such amiable characters as those of the abbess and sisters of the convent, the mind of the grateful Angela acquired a serenity, to which she had been long estranged; and the many days that elapsed between her parting with, and hearing from father Bernada, were far from heavy. The child of the ill-fated Julia acquired every hour a stronger hold on her affections: and the delight to which she looked forward in the conscious purity of her own mind, in the enjoyment of di Montmorenci's occasional society, when he should have learnt to consider her only as the sister his heart had selected, imparted a sunshine that gave brightness to the future. Thus had Angela passed a fortnight at the convent, when the following letter was delivered her from Father Bernado:

To Angela Moresco,

Prepare your mind, my good child, before you peruse what I am about to write, for the relation of an event at which your virtuous spirit will shrink: and be not shocked at learning, that by that event, you are released from those ties, so repugnant to your feelings, by the last act of guilt a sinner can commit. Moresco can no longer call on your obedience, his own hand, urged by a fear of mortal judgement, has precipitated him before the more awful tribunal of his offended creator. After leaving you, I applied to the Holy Inquisition, and accompanied by a party of officials, repaired to the Count Ruvello's: on enquiring for the count, we were shown into the saloon, where he was seated with the Signior Moresco, who wore the garb of a religious order; on our showing the order bearing the stamp of the holy office, the count turned deadly pale, and terrified by the acute enquiries of one of the officers, he endeavoured to screen himself by incriminating his companion; and in order to save his life, made an ample confession, by which means he made it clear by the evidence of his domestics, that he was at his own palace on the night the deed was committed. This confession, which I fear his cowardice more than his integrity induced him to make, was noted down by one of the officials, and signed by his own hand.

Moresco, surprised by the suddenness of the event, and struck with conscious guilt, was not prepared to defend the charge; and they were both confined in separate apartments under a strict guard. Their persons were searched, and everything of a suspicious nature taken from them; but Moresco, as it afterwards proved, carried a small and curiously constructed instrument so concealed, that it escaped detection, in case of his falling into the hands of justice, to rescue him from a more ignominious death; and finding an opportunity, he, unperceived, plunged it into his breast; after which, only signing the paper that spoke to the identity of the child, he refused to confess; and in a few hours expired. The Count Ruvello has since been conducted to the inquisition, where he was soon after brought to trial, and being found guilty on his own confession, his property was confiscated to the state, and himself banished.

I have only, my daughter, delayed sending you accounts before, because foreseeing the speedy termination of this important business, I was unwilling to disturb your quiet by unnecessarily sending you statements of its progress. It will be requisite that the child should be immediately returned to the seat of her ancestors, that her existence may be universally acknowledged; after which, as no guardian is provided for her infancy, you, who have so truly protected her, will be well entitled to the trust, provided it should be your wish to undertake the charge; and now, my virtuous daughter, I have only to communicate to you intelligence of a nature, that gives me great pleasure, presuming on your permission, to do what I thought best. I have revealed to his holiness the Pope, every circumstance relating to yourself since you quitted the Marchioness di Montmorenci's; not even concealing the cause of your departure, for it reflects great honour to your character. And the great and good man, in token of his approbation of your conduct, and his pity for your misfortunes, has bestowed on you the sum of two thousand crowns; causing at the same time so much of your tale to be made known, that your long absence may be accounted for, and that you may receive the esteem and respect of all, for the firmness and integrity of your conduct. I have nothing further to add than to assure you of my prayers to that Being, whose mercy is ever extended for the welfare of his creatures.

FATHER BERNADA

This important letter was followed by a mission from the Pope, entrusted with the deeds that secured to her the property he had awarded, and imparted his wish that she should accompany the child to the castle of its late parents, that she might be received and acknowledged by the vassals and domestics as their future mistress.

Angela immediately prepared for her departure, and accompanied by a suitable number of male and female attendants, who were sent to conduct her, she reached in safety the place of destination, from which in a few days she returned with her little charge to Santa Maria.

Di Montmorenci in the meanwhile, revering the delicacy of his Angela's mind, forbore for the present urging his claims on her heart; contenting himself with writing a congratulation on the honours she had received, and adding a hope, that she would allow him, at no very distant period, the happiness of seeing her. To this letter, Angela replied that her spirits had been so much agitated by the late events, that she felt it necessary to her health for some time to debar herself the gratification of seeing her friends; but she trusted in a few weeks to have the satisfaction which she had so long and anxiously desired. She found occasion to send a similar answer to many others who had taken a warm interest in her fate, and truly rejoiced in her restoration.

Di Montmorenci well understood the meaning of her reply, and feeling certain he had no cause to fear the duration of love in a mind like hers, he endeavoured to stifle his impatience. At length the happiness he sought was permitted him, and Angela received his occasional visits in the parlour of the convent. It was impossible for di Montmorenci to repeat these interviews, and to remain silent on a subject that so entirely filled his mind; and he at length ventured, after many indirect expressions, to decisively declare his wishes, and solicit a promised period for his happiness. Angela felt too sincere a love, and possessed too little affectation, to allow her to refuse an assurance there could be no impropriety in granting; and she consented to give her hand, when the twelve-months of her widowhood should have expired. And di Montmorenci, happy in the permission he had obtained, to see her once a week during the period of his probation, forbore to urge her for a nearer day.

Angela passed the year that intervened between the death of Moresco and her marriage with di Montmorenci at Santa Maria, to which she was doubly urged, by the pleasure she derived in the society of the sisterhood, and her wish to seclude herself from the world, till the singular incidents of the preceding year should become less the subject of conversation, and herself in consequence less an object of curiosity.

In the safe and happy asylum she had found, time glided cheerfully away, and her health and spirits recovered the injury they had experienced from the painful incidents she had encountered. At length the morning arrived in which di Montmorenci received the promised hand of his beloved Angela; the good Father Bernada officiated at the marriage, and truly did his heart participate in the happiness. The marquis and his fair bride, soon after the ceremony, set out with a splendid retinue for Venice, where the amiable Angela was received with the respect and esteem due to her rank as the Marchioness di Montmorenci, and to the virtues that had ever claimed affection in the humble and modest Angela Modeni.

V

THE LIFE AND HORRID ADVENTURES
OF THE CELEBRATED DR FAUSTUS

Anonymous

Stories based on famous characters of myth and legend were also
popular subjects in the supernatural 'bluebooks', and particularly
successful were those featuring the Wandering Jew, Dr Faustus
and, of course, the Devil himself. In all these books, the anonymous writers mixed fact and fiction with careless abandon and
were usually well served with vivid engravings. They were also
accorded very explicit title pages so that the reader could be in
no doubt as to the excitement to be found therein. The story
which I have selected, "The Life and Horrid Adventures of the
Celebrated Dr Faustus", published by Orlando Hodgson of Cloth
Fair, London, *circa* 1810, is typical of these, and beneath the
title ran the following lines, "Relating his First Introduction to
Lucifer, And Connection with Infernal Spirits; his Method of
Raising the Devil, And his Final Dismissal to the Tremendous
Abyss of Hell". Coupled with a lurid illustration of Faustus busy
summoning the Evil One, who could resist the shilling required
for its purchase?

*   *   *

JOHN FAUSTUS WAS by far the most learned man of his
day; his researches had no bounds, his mind was capacious, his
memory retentive, his wit pointed and ready, he was deeply skilled
in all the sciences, a proficient in every branch of literature, and
a complete master, not only of the dead, but of all living languages
of his time: this extraordinary man was of obscure birth; his
father, a poor and labouring husbandman, who resided in a small

hamlet, in the province of Weimar, in Germany: he had, however, the advantage of having a rich uncle living at Wittenberg, who, not being blessed with children, took the young FAUSTUS, adopted him, and made him heir to his property; thus, instead of being doomed to follow the plough-tail, to work hard early and late, and to live upon the most homely fare, our hero was destined to bask in the sunshine of affluence, to tread the flowery meads of learning, to drink at the immortal fount, to climb Helicon's banks, and thereby reach the temple of fame.

Young FAUSTUS, now become the favourite of his uncle, who had a good living in his gift, was, in order to qualify him for the station, sent to study divinity at the university of Wittenberg; the same at which "Hamlet, Prince of Denmark" was educated; and which is rendered immortal by the unmatched pen of our great Shakespeare. Here he prosecuted his studies until he had exhausted the stores of learning; he regularly passed his different examinations for the various minor academical degrees, with great credit to himself, and honour to his tutors—when at last he presented himself for the superior degree he was not according to the laws of the university of sufficient standing, but as he was known to be a man of a vast and comprehensive genius, stood unrivalled as a polemicist and, as none of his contemporaries were found qualified to hold theological argument with him, he was made an exception to the general rule, suffered to pass his final examination, and by unanimous consent, admitted as a Doctor of Divinity; being moreover considered as one whose brilliant talents and extensive education would shed a lustre on the city and university in which he had studied. He was inducted into his uncle's living, was looked up to as a most impressive and orthodox preacher, and might in time, had he been properly disposed, have risen to the highest clerical preferment; but, alas! his genius and his fortune were fated to take a different and less honourable direction: in short, the world was obliged to confess 'his talents great, but sorely misapplied'.

> Who guilty pleasures will pursue,
> In the end such conduct must rue;
> Nor wealth nor learning will avail,
> If vice triumphant swells the sail.

The DEVIL cunningly prepares,
And for his victims spreads his snares;
Thus FAUSTUS in a luckless hour,
Submitted was to Satan's pow'r.

For not content to be the first,
Amongst the learned and the just;
As needs must seek for to obtain,
That knowledge men will never gain.

FAUSTUS had virtuous relatives, who, seeing him possessed of strong natural abilities, with an aptitude for improvement; and having the means to provide handsomely for him in the church, were desirous to give play to his faculties, and to bring him up to religious studies; but FAUSTUS was blind to the generous feelings of his uncle, was deaf to the good wishes of his friends, and was moreover careless of his own reputation: for being evilly disposed, he addicted himself to the baneful study of necromancy, and the malignant arts of conjuration and soothsaying; aiming to see future events, to fathom the depths of nature, and pry into the inscrutable secret of hidden causes, in short, to discover the arcana of the universe: his companions were selected from the herd of impostors called Alchemists, who, to the disgrace of the ages, then infested every corner of Europe; from among astrologers as ignorant as they were presumptuous; in short, from among men, who outraged every feeling of decorum, and set themselves up as beings to whom everything was revealed and to whom nothing was unknown, except the road to virtue and honest industry: but FAUSTUS was not a man long to be deceived by such impudent pretenders; his quick and penetrating genius soon enabled him to discover their ignorant assurance, and although he quitted them with scorn, as unworthy of his notice, he did not abandon his own wicked pursuit for distinction in the devilish arts of magic and witchcraft; on the contrary, he followed them up with more ardency than ever, frequently falling into the deepest reveries, and was often so absorbed by his cogitations, that he became a by-word among the students, who nicknamed him the *speculator*: at first he indulged his theoretical dreams in private; but at length he grew callous to public opinion, and openly casting from him the scriptures, in derision of his profession as a priest; began, to the great mortification of his uncle, who would fain have reclaimed him, to lead a most dissolute and ungodly life: he practised as a physician, giving his advice gratis to all comers, among whom he effected the most miraculous cures, for it is an unquestionable fact, that his knowledge of the healing art was most consummate, and that he had by his elaborate researches, become better acquainted with the medicinal virtues of herbs and minerals, than any other practitioner of his day. FAUSTUS turned a deaf ear to advice of all kinds, and looking more to the joys of the world than to the value of his soul, he preferred the present to the future; continued his abominable course with a fixed determination, if possible, to become acquainted with the great secret of the original formation of the world.

> How all was made, from whence all came,
> Requires more wit than man can claim,
> To see the future too we find,
> Exceeds the wisdom of mankind;
> Yet FAUSTUS fain these things would know,
> And his superior learning show;
> For this regardless of the evil,
> He made a compact with the DEVIL:
> Just so, the child who breaks his toy
> That he the inside may enjoy;
> Finds out too late, and to his cost,
> He has but learnt his toy is lost.

FAUSTUS, now resolute to rank first in the magical art, furnished himself with all the books he could find, that embraced the subjects of his meditation; these he studied day and night, until he became so familiar with the mysteries of the black art, the figures and characters of enchantments, invocations to spirits, and every other knowledge requisite to the preparation of incantations, that he surpassed all those with whom he conversed; indeed he was fond of exhibiting before them such things as left them in utter astonishment. Having proceeded thus far, he became more impatient for the accomplishment of his favourite object; and began to entertain the notion of calling the Devil to his assistance; no sooner did this purpose enter his head, than he began to make preparations for carrying it into effect; to raise the Devil therefore, he adopted all the means of which he was master.

On consulting his oracles, he found it was requisite to undergo a probation of forty days, during which he must five times every day invoke the prince of darkness; trample on the holy Bible, seclude himself from society, and drink morning and evening, repeating his diabolical lessons, two spoonsful of Devil's soup: he drew a magical circle upon the floor of his apartment, and then with diligence, set about getting together the materials for his infernal diet; this was both a work of time and labour, as many of the ingredients were extremely difficult to be procured; to make and eat his hellish mixture required however no common degree of fortitude, but he had taken his resolution, and therefore he began to rummage the churchyards for human bones of a particular description, in the hollows of which worms of a certain shape and colour had engendered; he then procured newts of a month old; the eyes of dead brindled sows; eagles' eggs with five black spots on them; hoofs of cows that had died of the murrain; heads and legs of toads; spawn of frogs; genitals of scorpions; tongues of crocodiles; livers of male black rats; toes of nightingales, brains of white boars above three years old; and spurs of game cocks; the whole of this was boiled to a consistence with whale's sperm and snails; to which he added every morning seventy-three drops of his own blood, taken from his left arm by himself.

Having concocted this devilish potion, he in all things conformed himself to his probationary state, tearing Bibles to pieces and treading the scattered leaves under his feet: towards the end of the time uncommon noises began to assail his ears, whilst he was taking the abominable soup, and whenever he poured his blood into it, the room would suddenly fill with dense clouds of smoke, having a sulphurous smell; singing and music was heard as at a distance; at other times moaning cries resembling those of new-born infants as if suffering pain, would as if they were in the chamber; then suddenly, heavy groans would arise as if someone was dying beneath the flooring; at another time it would appear as if the trampling of a thousand horses was mounting the stairs; then the windows would rattle, and all the doors in the house clap: by these tokens, FAUSTUS well knew he was rapidly advancing towards his wishes, and therefore when the forty days were expired, he resolved to put all to the hazard, and use the utmost powers of his art to bring Belzebub into his presence.

All things being in readiness, FAUSTUS repaired about midnight to a thick wood near Wittenberg, and selecting an open spot where four cross roads met, he drew a circle on the ground, round which he traced various cabalistic figures; and sprinkled it over with a hundred drops of his own blood, taken from his left arm; he then placed within the circle a little globe covered with magical characters, and a magical bowl containing some of the soup; he next covered his head with a woollen cap, on which were painted a death's head and cross bones, together with a figure of the Devil; then throwing into the circle the fragments of the holy Bible, he resolutely took his stand within it, and fearlessly waving his wand, he began to invoke the demon, using the following words: "*Mitgchen vater toufel ganz rasenel, werden veru andeln allwo kliener teufel forts chicksen abgesandter.*" He had no sooner uttered this, than a thick smoke like burning sulphur filled the whole forest, and was so offensive that it almost choked him. FAUSTUS however stood firm, it then began to thunder as if the world were at an end, and the lightning so constant and so vivid, and the flashes succeeded each other so rapidly, that the wood appeared as if it was burning in all directions, or rather, as if it were one solid mass of fire; the most horrid noises were heard; the most piercing screams followed in quick succession: then was heard the roaring of lions, the yell of tigers, and the growling of bears, as if the forest were filled with wild beasts; then came the rumbling of stones, as if thousands of men were rolling huge masses down the paved sides of a steep hill; next came a discharge of cannon, so loud and so strong, that all the artillery in the universe, if fired at the same time, could have produced nothing like it, so fearful and terrifying did it sound: FAUSTUS manfully maintained his post, and taking up the magical bowl of soup, he drank it and danced on the leaves of the Bible; suddenly the most delicious music sprung up, as if some thousands of the sweetest instruments were sounded; then he heard the singing of women so delightfully soft and melodious, that it quite ravished his senses; at this moment a frightful dragon hovered in the air over his head, holding a three-pronged pitchfork, and vomiting fire; the music ceased and the most hellish noises succeeded, when to his astonishment, FAUSTUS saw a hare chasing a lion; a sparrow pursuing an eagle; a man fighting with a tiger; a hyena swallowing up little children; and all appeared to be making directly towards the circle: he however was nothing daunted but kept on repeating his invocation, when the dragon falling to the ground, a smart little man dressed in black with a cocked hat on his head came forward and said, *"Friend* FAUSTUS, *what wantest thou, Lucifer my master has sent me here to know?"* FAUSTUS keeping his ground, repeated the charm, danced over the fragments of the holy Bible, and said with a stern voice, "Tell thy master that my business is with him, and that I must and will see him, though he were buried in fifty hells deeper than he is." The storm recommenced more furiously than ever, and at last there fell very near him a great ball of fire, which kept running round and round the circle with incredible velocity, sending forth the most appalling noises, and such a horrid smell, he was almost suffocated; FAUSTUS however was not afraid: at length, a voice like thunder was heard to say, *"Mortal, what wantest thou, that thus you disturb my repose?"* FAUSTUS firmly answered, "Belzebub, come forth, and let us drink together, out of thine own liquor, which I have here with me," repeating his invocation as before; then there came such a tremendous clap of thunder, that FAUSTUS was stunned by it, and for the first time felt the sensation of fear; he however steadily kept his place within the circle, and recruited himself with a spoonful of soup: at that moment the storm suddenly subsided, and soft music was again heard: the ball of fire opened, and there issued the DEVIL in his own proper person, who civilly said *"Faustus, thou art a bold man, and hast prevailed unhappily for thyself: what wantest thou with me?"* FAUSTUS then gave him the magical bowl of soup, out of which the devil drank, and said, *"wilt thou be mine, soul and body for ever, Faustus?"* "No, demon," replied FAUSTUS courageously, "I will not! I will have all I desire of thee, and yet I will not be damned!" "FAUSTUS," said the DEVIL, *"that cannot be, damned thou art already by what thou hast done; however, I am willing for thy boldness to hear what it is thou wanted me to do for thee; and for that purpose I leave my faith-*

ful servant MEPHOSTOPHILES *with thee, write thy wishes on this skin, it once covered a human body, and one of thine own ancestors; write I say on this skin thy propositions, but mind, let it be in thine own blood, taken from thy left arm; give it to the spirit, he will convey it to me, and thou shalt have my answer; but remember, in all transactions with thee, I will have them recorded and written with thine own blood; and now wretched man, fare thee well; soon, very soon, we shall be closer connected, for thou wilt reside with me in hell.*" So saying, he vanished, and FAUSTUS found himself standing in his circle in the wood with the little man, who was the spirit MEPHOSTOPHILES: he desired his little friend to call upon him the next day for his propositions, to which the spirit assented, telling him that he now knew the way to make either him or his master attend him: FAUSTUS then returned home, well pleased with the success of his enterprise; flattering himself that he should gain his own ends, and at last outwit the DEVIL; but in this he grossly deceived himself.

FAUSTUS was in his study, ruminating how he might get his desires fulfilled by the DEVIL, and yet avoid damnation; when MEPHOSTOPHILES stood before him, saying *"Master, behold I am here to do thy bidding, and receive thy propositions to the Prince of Pandemonium."* FAUSTUS, who had employed himself all the morning in writing them, gave them to him, and the room filling with a sulphurous smoke, the spirit vanished: these were the nine propositions which he made to the DEVIL.

PROPOSITIONS OF FAUSTUS TO THE DEVIL

FIRST: That from this moment, until the hour of my death, the Devil either by himself or his agents, shall at all times, and in all seasons, be at my command, and come to me in any shape or form that I may require.

SECOND: That he shall do my bidding without a murmur, whether by night or by day, be obedient to me in all things, and reveal to me all the secrets of nature; how everything came, and where from.

THIRD: That whenever I require a supply of money or jewels, he shall furnish me with them forthwith, to whatever extent I may require.

FOURTH: That whatever I may desire or ask for, shall be brought to me without delay.

FIFTH: That whenever or wherever I may choose to travel, whether to the remotest part of the world, to the tops of the highest mountains, to any other planet, or into the regions of air, he shall either by himself or his spirits, conduct me without loss of time, or the knowledge of any one.

SIXTH: That he shall render me invisible, whenever I may feel inclined to be so.

SEVENTH: That he shall when required, bring before me the image of any person, however long that person has been dead.

EIGHTH: That he shall show me the interior of hell, and explain all its mysteries, and the nature of its government.

NINTH: That he shall above all things when conversing with me, either by himself or his subordinate spirits, lay aside his devilish propensity to lying, and tell me nothing but the truth, and moreover, that he shall give me true answers to all my questions.   JOHN FAUSTUS

MEPHOSTOPHILES was not long in bringing back the answer: a terrible clap of thunder that shook the house to its foundation announced his approach, when he presented FAUSTUS with a scroll, on which was written,

REPLY FROM THE DEVIL TO DOCTOR FAUSTUS

First Proposition—granted; provided you require no religious ceremony, and that you bind yourself in a bond, which shall be dictated by my spirit MEPHOSTOPHILES to renounce heaven and religion for ever.

Second Proposition—granted with this reserve, that I can only tell you what I myself know.

Third Proposition—granted freely: provided the bond be given, making over your soul and body to me for ever.

Fourth Proposition—granted: provided it be upon the face of the earth.

Fifth Proposition—granted: with the exception of the other planets.

Sixth Proposition—granted.

Seventh Proposition—granted.

Eighth Proposition—granted as far as showing the place, which is needless, as you will so soon live entirely in it.

Ninth Proposition—I will answer only such questions as I may be able to do, but when I do answer, I will, as I always do, answer them truly—the world does me an injustice, to tax me with want of veracity, 'tis their own evil disposition makes them think so ill of me, let them ask their conscience if ever I deceived them, or made them believe a bad action was a good one.

Moreover, I hereby promise to let my trusty servant MEPHOSTOPHILES, be ever at your call, and further allow you twenty-four years to enjoy the privileges you have purchased at so dear a rate—Signed by order of Lucifer, Prince of the hellish regions, by us the judges of his infernal domain; and in his name we say amen, it shall be so.

RHADAMANTHUS
MINOS
EACUS

FAUSTUS changed colour when he read the scroll, he clearly saw the Devil was too many for him, but he had proceeded too far to recede; besides he still relied upon the potency of his charms to effect all he wanted, and was so infatuated as to suppose he should yet contrive some means to save his soul, and escape the dreadful alternative upon which he was to receive the DEVIL'S assistance: he therefore began to parley with MEPHOSTOPHILES, endeavouring to evade giving the bond required; but the spirit was immovable, threatening to leave him, and refused to do anything until the bond was regularly drawn and signed; FAUSTUS, being determined to pursue his own plans rather than fail, agreed to the terms, and the following bonds were then written upon two human skins, which, as the spirit said, had belonged to his relatives.

BOND FROM FAUSTUS TO THE DEVIL

I, JOHN FAUSTUS, of the university of Wittenberg, in Germany, Doctor of Divinity, and student in Astrology, being in perfect health, do of my own free will and pleasure, and without any restraint whatever, openly declare, that although I have diligently applied myself to the study of natural causes, and to the investigation of the elements of nature and their causes, yet that I am not satisfied with the lights and understanding granted me by heaven, which are not adequate to bring me to the extent of my desires, and that I have not been able to find any man with sufficient learning and penetration to instruct me further in the means by which I may obtain the object of my ambition.

Being unwilling to relinquish this pursuit, and fully determined at all hazards, and at whatever risk or cost to accomplish my purpose—I DOCTOR JOHN FAUSTUS, finding that none other except the DEVIL himself can bring me to the desired end, have entered into a solemn agreement with the Prince of darkness, monarch of the infernal regions, commonly called the DEVIL, through the medium of his messenger and agent MEPHOSTO-PHILES, one of the infernal spirits, serving his infernal Majesty, that provided he the DEVIL shall yield me all due obedience, and fulfil my desires in all things in that case, I shall bind myself, both body and soul to him for ever and ever, and renounce heaven, salvation, religion and all religious ceremonies.

Therefore, provided his Satanic Majesty does for the full space of twenty-four years, to be reckoned from the day of the date hereof, faithfully serve me, and the twenty-four years convenanted for being fully expired, I, DOCTOR JOHN FAUSTUS, do by these presents, resign myself, my soul, my body, my goods, and all that may belong to me, without reserve, to him the DEVIL, and do invest him with full power over me, to send for, fetch or carry me alive or dead, to whatever place he may choose, and hereupon I defy all the host of heaven and all living creatures, whether man or beast, and in his name I say amen, it shall be so.

And that this intrument may have its proper force, and not be liable to any evasion, I hereby again renounce heaven and all its glory, for the darkness of the infernal regions, and have thereunto written and signed it with a pen dipped in my own blood, drawn from my left arm, and mixed with boiling brimstone brought by MEPHOSTOPHILES from hell, and I call upon the whole host of Devils to witness my signature.

JOHN FAUSTUS

When this dreadful instrument was signed, the spirit MEPHOSTO-PHILES said his instructions were on the part of the DEVIL, to give him a counter bond, "*for his master,*" he said, was "*one of the most honourable beings existing,*" and he accordingly wrote the following:

Bond from Mephostophiles to Doctor John Faustus

I, MEPHOSTOPHILES, one of the infernal spirits, and agent to the great Lucifer, Prince of darkness, and monarch of the infernal regions, do hereunto agree on the part of his Satanic Majesty, with JOHN FAUSTUS, of the university of Wittenberg, in Germany, Doctor of Divinity, that his said Majesty shall duly and truly serve, or cause to be served, the said DOCTOR JOHN FAUSTUS, for and during the full space and term of twenty-four years, to be reckoned from the day of the date hereof, according to the reply made to nine propositions, of him the said FAUSTUS, written with his own blood, copies of which are hereby annexed; and that at the expiration of the said term, he the said JOHN FAUSTUS, shall become both soul and body, whether alive or dead, the whole and sole property of my said master the DEVIL, and further that I will attend the said JOHN FAUSTUS personally, whenever called on during the whole of the said term, and do his bidding as far as is consistent with the tenor of his Satanic Majesty's reply, in witness whereof, I have signed this Instru-ment in his presence, with a pen dipped in a composition made of boiling brimstone brought by me from hell, and the blood of the said FAUSTUS, drawn by himself from his left arm, and in my master the DEVIL'S name I say amen, it shall be so.

MEPHOSTOPHILES

The bonds being mutually exchanged, the spirit MEPHOSTO-PHILES addressed him familiarly, saying, "*Come, my FAUSTUS, be of good cheer, man, although thou hath damned thyself to all eternity for a few years of pleasure, yet thou shall lead a merry life for the time; and be the envy and admiration of the world.*" Then putting a large key into his hand, he continued, "*Take this, it is the key of one of the gates of Hell, and a favour never before granted to mortal: whenever you wish to see me, if you hold up this key above your head with your right hand, and say*

GLISHMARAMROTH TEUFEL, *I shall instantly appear in the shape you now see me,*" which was as before described in the form of a dapper little man, neatly dressed in black, with a cocked hat on his head, looking much like a French Abbé.

FAUSTUS having thus succeeded in accomplishing the great purpose he had in view, prepared to avail himself of his power, and to seek distinction as well for his wealth and splendour, as for his superior knowledge; accordingly he bought a large stately mansion that had once been a palace belonging to one of the Caesars; money being no longer any object with him, he furnished it in a style of the greatest magnificence, filled his cellars with the choicest and most costly wines, purchased a superb service of massy gold plate, hired a complete set of servants suitable to his establishment, set up a splendid equipage, and began to live like a nobleman of the first rank: and had the finest stud of horses that was to be found in all Germany, with hounds and dogs of all descriptions.

FAUSTUS, who was a man of some humour, now began to amuse himself with the exercise of his devilish powers: sometimes he would disguise himself and go round to the different gaming houses, and by the aid of his familiar, win all the money, let them play for whatever they might: one night, when there was a very large company assembled, having played until he had won everything as usual, he suddenly rendered himself invisible, and then ordered MEPHOSTOPHILES to set the cards and dice a-dancing over the tables and about the room, and at the same time to make them squeak just like pigs under the knife of the butcher; this so terrified the company, that they ran out of the house, swearing that either the DEVIL or DOCTOR FAUSTUS was there; but judge their surprise, when each on reaching his own home, found the exact money he had lost lying on the table in his bed chamber; when he went to take it up, he was prevented by a little dog jumping up and snapping at his fingers: sometimes he would call at a friend's house, and while he was talking to the family, would cause sweet music, just as if someone was playing in the room either upon a guitar, flute, harpsichord, violin, French horn or clarinet, according as fancy happened to strike him; then suddenly change it into the cry of a pack of hounds, or the chattering of a score of magpies: these and a thousand other tricks of the kind he was continually playing: an old woman once offended him, and he revenged himself in a curious manner as she was one day sitting down to a hot dinner of something she was very fond of; the dish suddenly disappeared, and a gentle sprinkling of water as if thrown up by a fountain kept flowing over her, she ran from one room to another thinking to avoid the wetting, but go where she would although nothing was to be seen, the water kept playing over her without intermission for three days and three nights; what most astonished her and all her acquaintances was that, although her clothes were wet to her skin, yet the moment she pulled them off they were perfectly dry, and notwithstanding great crowds came to see her in this situation, yet no one received a drop of the water but herself; the poor old woman was dreadfully alarmed, and very unhappy at her miserable condition, when suddenly the sprinkling ceased, and the dinner of which she had been thus disappointed, reappeared upon the table as hot as ever, and at the exact hour she had sat down to it three days before; but to her great surprise and satisfaction, round the edges of the dish were placed twenty pieces of gold money of different countries; these when she attempted to touch them, leaped off the dish and rolled round the room, the old woman running after them, when in a moment she lost sight of them; but happening to put her hand into her pocket, she found them all safely there. He once set all the clocks (of which there was an immense number kept in the town of Wittenberg) crowing at the same time, and they continued their shrill clarion notes for three hours without intermission, to the great dismay and wonder of the inhabitants, who could by no means account for so extraordinary an occurrence: at another time, just as the parson had mounted the pulpit in the great church, he got all the pigs within six miles of the place to come suddenly to the church; they began grunting and squeaking and so continued until the time for divine service had expired, and the congregation were obliged to go home without hearing either prayers or sermon, for fear of spoiling their dinners.

Among other pranks he once so contrived it, that at a certain hour in the day, all the old maids in Wittenberg should be seen walking one after the other down one side of the street, with each a penny pie in her hand, and a tabby cat by her side, while at the same time, all the old bachelors were seen walking down the other, each having a knife and fork in his hand, with a clean napkin under his arm, the men bowing, the women curtseying, attended by an immense crowd of men, women and children, laughing and joking; and it was so arranged, although unknown to each other, that they should all be dressed alike, the men in one costume, the women in another; they would fain have retired, but so potent was the charm, it was not until they had traversed the whole city, that they had power to separate.

One Christmas night, he so ordered it, that all the clothing of the inhabitants, not only that which they had in wear, but all that was in the drawers, should be taken from them while asleep, and hid in the cellars, and that each should in this condition be taken from their own house, and removed into some neighbour's bed, so arranging it, that where it was possible the change should be among those of the same trade or profession; in the morning, they found themselves each in a strange house, stark naked, and without any clothes to put on; they were most ludicrously situated, for if they sent for a tailor, the answer was. "*I am naked, and cannot come.*" The mantua makers and milliners were obliged to send the same answer, and the servants being naked like their masters and mistresses, would not attend, alleging the same excuse.

Amidst all this festivity, FAUSTUS wanted someone who would participate with him in his enjoyments; he determined to marry, and communicated with his familiar; but he no sooner broached the subject, than he replied, "*My* FAUSTUS, *thou canst not marry; remember, marriage is a religious ceremony, and thou hast sworn to defy religion and all its rights, as we do.*" FAUSTUS too plainly saw that he could by no artifice deceive the Devil, and he said,— "It shall be so; I will think no more of marriage." "*It is a wise determination, my Faustus,*" replied the spirit, "*thou doest well to keep to the tenor of thy agreement.*"

Sometime after, he called Lucifer to him in person, and addressed him, "Friend DEVIL, I find I cannot resist the inclination I have to marry, for I am unable to bridle my fancy; I therefore must and will have a wife; I pray thee to grant thy consent": he had hardly finished, before the most hideous noises were heard, clashing of swords and firing of pistols; the room filled with a black sulphurous smoke that stank most abominably, a tremendous clap of thunder rocked the mansion to its foundation, dragons with pitchforks vomiting flames seemed placed on all sides of him; a cock and a hen appeared to be fighting a desperate battle; and he felt as if his flesh was pinched by a thousand devils; in vain he attempted to fly, he was stopped and thrown backwards and forwards like a football so that he was thoroughly alarmed, and called to MEPHOSTOPHILES for help; in his place came a Devil, with a most frightful countenance. FAUSTUS could scarcely muster courage sufficient to look the monster in the face; at last he asked him who he was, and what he wanted: "*I am,*" replied the demon, grinning horribly, and holding out a scourge made of iron wire, heated red hot, "*one of Hell's executioners, my name is* GHASTOMIO, *I am sent to enquire what are now thy thoughts about marriage, how thou likest thy wedding, and what further thou wouldst have?*" FAUSTUS now acknowledged his error.

GHASTOMIO said, "*Know, rebellious mortal, that Lucifer my master is generous and can forgive, but will not be trifled with; you must not indulge in freaks of this kind, with impunity*". MEPHOSTOPHILES then making his appearance, said, "*Let me give thee a piece of wholesome advice, my* FAUSTUS, *there is no jesting with us; hold faithfully to the terms of thy bond, and thou shalt have no cause of complaint: my master has instructed me to say, that he admires thy daring spirit: that therefore thou shalt have thy heart's desire of what woman soever thou wilt.*" FAUSTUS was mightily pleased with this, and began to think he was a great fool to think of marrying.

FAUSTUS now resumed his wonted humour; having dined with a large party, they took a stroll in the evening and met a farmer's man driving a load of hay: FAUSTUS, determined to have some fun, accosted the man, saying, "That seems nice hay you have there, my honest fellow, how much must I give you to eat my belly full of it?" The man stared at him, thinking he was beside himself to talk of eating hay; however, the countryman was inclined to humour the joke, and agreed with him for a penny, which honest John thought would be all clear gain; however, he was much deceived in his calculation, for FAUSTUS fell to, and appeared to eat so ravenously, that more than half the load presently disappeared: at this the man scratching his head, said with a melancholy voice, "*Ads wounds maister, I pray ye now leave off, an ye be not minded to ruin a poor man; ods bodikens, now who would have thoughten you would have eaten the hay.*" His company could not help laughing, and FAUSTUS jocularly said, "Well my honest lad, remember another time how you sell your master's hay, I could eat it all, but I have compassion on thee, so go thy ways whilst one half thy load is safe." The man drove on, cursing his own folly and the eater of his hay: however, when he came home, he was surprised to find that not any of his hay was wanting, and more pleased when, on putting his hand into his pocket, he found five guineas.

FAUSTUS was famed far and near; his almanacks were a constant theme of praise; whatever he predicted, as wind, hail, frost, snow, rain, it occurred as he predicted.

FAUSTUS, being in want of money, went into his great hall, and holding up his magical key, summoned his familiar; addressing him, he said, "How is it, that thou performest not thy promise to me?" The spirit replied, "*Master, in nothing have I neglected thee; I know thy thoughts, and am not unmindful of thy wants.*" The spirit disappeared amidst loud claps of thunder: FAUSTUS found standing in one corner of the hall, three immense sacks, one filled with the rarest jewels, another with gold, and the third with silver.

FAUSTUS now prepared to travel, and summoned MEPHOSTOPHILES; it was agreed that he should visit the courts of all the monarchs in the world, and play some merry pranks at each: they accordingly set off; when they came to the frontiers of Russia, the custom-house officers congratulated themselves on their good luck, for the carriage appeared to be stuffed full of contraband goods; FAUSTUS offered them a small bribe, which he well knew they would refuse, in hopes of getting a larger; he then said to them, "Well then, you must do your duty"; they began joyfully to unpack, but no sooner had they touched them, than the most abominable stench issued forth, so that they were almost poisoned; an unseen hand suddenly applied a hot trowel to their backsides, while a growling bear seized them by the nose with a pair of sharp pincers.

At a grand levee held by the Emperor of China, when the Mandarins and nobles were assembled, they all suddenly began hissing like so many serpents, and doubling their fists ran furiously about, threatening to knock each other down; the Emperor himself began to blow his nose so incessantly, and at each time there issued such a number of curious worms and butterflies, that the palace was quickly filled, the one flying up to the ceilings, the others crawling upon the walls and floors; during this confusion, FAUSTUS caused them all to appear as if they had changed heads, when each seeing his own head upon another man's shoulders, ran home terrified out their senses. At a sumptuous repast given by the King of Persia, FAUSTUS caused every man's wine suddenly to spring up from the bottle like a fountain and fill his glass, which he no sooner put to his mouth, than it flowed back again through the bottom into the decanter, so that no one could get any wine that day. At the court of the great Mogul, when the Mogul and his counsellors of state were in deep debate, he caused the whole to begin sneezing and pinching his neighbour's ears, so that they could not do any business. At a grand ball given by the Spanish Monarch, he caused the ladies while dancing, suddenly to draw up one leg under their petticoats, and keep dancing on the other, while the gentlemen deliberately pulled off their coats and wigs.

In the course of his travels, he visited India, Persia, China, Europe and Africa; ascended the highest mountains; being on Mount Caucassus, he expressed a desire to behold the place from whence our first parents were driven, when MEPHOSTOPHILES taking him up into the air, "Yonder," said he, "is Paradise, the garden planted by God himself; those four mighty streams are rivers flowing out of it, and yonder stands angel Michael with the flaming sword; nor wilt thou nor any other mortal, not even my master, Lucifer, nor any of his spirits be ever permitted to approach nearer than thou doest at this moment."

FAUSTUS, resuming his old theme, was desirous of becoming acquainted with the secret of the formation of the universe, for this purpose he made use of his key: "Pray inform me," said he, "in what way God made the world, and all the creatures in it, and why he made man after his own image." The spirit looking maliciously at him, replied, "Wherefore asketh thou this, well thou knowest I cannot answer thee, for we know not ourselves, this is contrary to thy bond: I know thou repentest of what thou hast done, but it availeth thee nothing now; and if thou continuest such questions, thou wilt be torn into atoms." Saying this, he vanished in a rage; suddenly *Lucifer* himself appeared, accompanied by many infernal demons, in hideous shapes.

"FAUSTUS," said the DEVIL, looking fiercely at him, "*what is* it thou wouldst have? I know well thy thoughts, thou wouldst evade thy promise," and here he produced the bond, "but know, wretched mortal, that nothing can save thee from my fury; wilt thou remain contented with the terms of our agreement, or shall I punish thee for thy attempt at evasion? Speak, my servants are ready, and they will soon show you some of our hellish pastimes, here is thy old acquaintance, GHASTOMIO, wouldst thou like that he should handle thee a little?" At this the demons began to brandish their weapons, and to howl hideously; FAUSTUS, falling prostrate, said in a melancholy tone, "Satan, I worship thee, and thee only; I renounce religion, God, his holy scriptures, and his mercy." The demons then disappeared, and the DEVIL taking FAUSTUS by the hand, cried, "It is enough, we will be friends; for, remember thy time has now but seven years to run, and I am willing that thou shouldst make the most of it."

FAUSTUS said to MEPHOSTOPHILES, "Inform me, I pray thee, what sort of a place hell is, where it is placed, how it is governed, and when it was made, and if it be possible for the damned ever to come again into the favour of God?" The spirit looking archly at him, replied, "My lord FAUSTUS, that is a secret thou wilt very soon become acquainted with; I will give thee the best description of it I am able; know then, that before the fall of my lord and master, Lucifer, there was no hell; it is an unfathomed gulf, raging with perpetual and inextinguishable fire, burning with brimstone, that is to endure to all eternity; where the souls of the damned lie broiling without hopes of mercy, and whose torments will never cease; these are sometimes tossed about from demon to demon with red hot pitchforks; there are a great variety of punishments inflicted on the wicked who are sent there—we have a man who is chained to a rock, and a vulture keeps perpetually gnawing his liver, which regenerates as fast as the vulture consumes it; he was on earth, called PROMETHEUS, his crime was, making the figure of a man, and then calling down fire from heaven to animate it—another is doomed to eternally roll an immense stone, which he moves with great labour up a hill, this, when he nearly reaches the summit, rolls down again to the bottom, in spite of all his efforts, and he is compelled to re-commence his arduous and never-ending task, his name is SISYPHUS;—another is IXION, fastened to a wheel, upon which he is to be eternally broken, without being permitted to end his sufferings; be again received into the favour of God, how would the knowledge of this avail thee, seeing thou hast by the bond for ever renounced God's mercy."

FAUSTUS now began to amuse himself by changing his shape; he would find out where a large party of ladies were assembled, and creeping into the room in the shape of a mouse, frighten them almost to death, by running up and down under their petticoats; when hunted and hard pressed, he would turn himself into a fly or a little dog, and thus escape: he has been known to get into the tribunals of justice in the form of a magpie, and flying over the judges and counsellors, pluck off their wigs, throw them on a heap on the floor, and smite upon their heads, to the amusement of the spectators. He ordered his familiar to procure twelve of the handsomest women in the world, with these he established a harem, and lived with them until the day of his death.

The following letter was published after his death, said to be written by FAUSTUS to a physician at Leipzig.

As you have expressed a wish to become acquainted with some of my extraordinary travels, I here send you an account of the most remarkable I ever made: one night, I looked out of my window and saw hovering in the air, a most splendid little open car, surrounded by a most brilliant flame, drawn by six of the most beautiful peacocks my eyes ever beheld; their tails were fully spread, and they were attached by silken cords to the car, which from its polish, resembled a looking-glass; it was attended by a griffin, who said, *"Mortal, fear nothing, I am the spirit* TRISMAGOMA, *sent to show thee the planets, but I dare not enter one of them: so take courage, make ready, jump into the car, and let's away."* We mounted in the air, and were far beyond the precincts of our world, when TRISMAGOMA pointed to a large ball, saying, "Mortal, that is the planet MERCURY, the people there are so curiously formed, that they coil themselves up like hedge-hogs, and roll from place to place instead of walking." The next we saw the planet VENUS; there he said, "the women ruled everything, had eyes at their fingers ends, with the most sparkling diamonds growing from their noses; they do not spoil their figures by bearing children, but lay eggs, which they ripen in the sun." We now came to the planet MARS; in that, said he, "The inhabitants are all soldiers, and continually fighting; they never beget children, but taking up the dead carcases of the slain, and hanging them upon polished ivory pegs, they come to life again, fully accoutred and equipped ready for actual service." The next was the planet JUPITER; this he told me, "was governed by VULCAN, who had immense forges, at which his Cyclops, men with but one eye in the centre of their forehead, are continually at work; everything, even men, women and children, is made of polished steel, and moved by clockwork; they are fed with paper, of which there are innumerable manufactories: an angel goes to the poles every morning and winds them up for the day, which is equal to twelve of our years: when they die, they are sent to the forges, and new ones made of the old materials." We now approached a very large one, which he said was SATURN. "There, the people are so rich, that they keep their carriages, and so plentiful is gold, that the streets are paved with it; the rats are so large, that they are used instead of coach-horses; monkeys build carpenters' shops, make bricks, do all the labour, and act as servants; it is full of peacocks, who, when the season is over for laying eggs, void the largest and most brilliant polished diamonds, which are cut into glass windows; oysters grow to the size of turtles, and are filled with very large and beautiful pearls, which are used to cover the heads of nails; heavy dews fall in the night, which clinging to the branches of the trees, are ripened by the sun into topazes, rubies, and emeralds. When they marry, the bride is wrapped up in a paste made of cobblers' wax and honey, of which there are immense lakes, then baked, and in that form presented to the happy bridegroom; they always spend their honeymoon on the roofs of their houses, watching the cats fight." He now pointed to a planet larger than any we had seen, and to four smaller ones; those, said he, "are not yet known to your earth, and therefore it will be needless to describe them"; then drawing near the earth, we sailed round it, and returned.

The term granted to FAUSTUS having expired, MEPHOSTOPHILES appeared to him, and showing him his bond, commanded him to make preparation, for the DEVIL would fetch him according to their stipulation: FAUSTUS changed colour, sighed and wept bitterly; on which his familiar addressed him briskly, saying, *"Come, come, my FAUSTUS, you have had your career, and a lewd and merry one it has been; do not act the coward at last."*

On the fatal day that was to terminate his career, he made a grand entertainment; after the banquet, he thus addressed them. "My well-beloved friends, as I must in a few hours for ever quit the world and its pleasures, I have brought you here that I may explain the mystery of my life: four-and-twenty years are now unhappily passed, since I entered into a compact with the DEVIL, by whose help I have performed all those wonderful things that have gained me so much renown and envy; I pledged to him my soul and body in lieu of the riches and pleasures he was to provide me; this night our compact finishes, and he has warned me that he will claim the fulfillment of my agreement.

"Now, although I have made such a wicked use of that fine understanding which it pleased God to bestow upon me, I most heartily repent of my evil courses, and as I wish to die in peace with all men, I have brought you hither that we may take a friendly, and I fear, everlasting farewell; and to entreat that you will hold up my wicked and abominable life, as a warning to others never to cease having THE FEAR OF GOD BEFORE THEIR EYES; and now my good friends, retire to your beds, and do not trouble yourselves about me, seeing that nothing can avert my unhappy fate: if, which I much fear is not likely, you should find my dead body, lay it decently in the earth, for I can truly say, *I die both a good and a bad Christian;* and write on my tombstone, HERE LIES FAUSTUS THE WICKED, WHO, TO GRATIFY HIS EVIL PROPENSITIES, SOLD HIMSELF TO THE DEVIL."

As the clock struck twelve, the DEVIL and GHASTOMIO appeared; FAUSTUS made a stout resistance uttering the most piercing cries, but the demons soon mastered him, when the latter taking him upon his pitchfork, flew away with him amidst a dreadful storm of thunder and lightning.

In the morning, his friends looked everywhere for his body, but it could nowhere be found; the only marks of him were some brains cleaving to the walls, his eyes, some of his teeth, and the hall sprinkled all over with his blood.

THE BLUEBOOK ILLUSTRATIONS

*A selection of engravings
from the 'Shilling Shockers'*

Crude illustration ftom "The Monk; Or, Father Innocent, Abbot of
the Capuchins" a chapbook plagiarism of Matthew Lewis's "The
Monk." Thomas Tegg, 1803.

"The Victim of Monkish Cruelty", a typical engraving from one of
Thomas Tegg's popular 'Shilling Shockers' (1803).

An ill-used 'bluebook' heroine in the inevitable state of disarray—from "The Distressed Nun" by Isaac Crookenden (1802).

The discovery of the imprisoned nun, Constance, in "The Mysterious Novice" by Sarah Wilkinson (1809).

A bandit captain confronted by the beautiful ghost of one of his victims: the frontispiece to "New Collection of Gothic Stories" (1801).

A sword-waving skeleton—one of the ghastly figures found in "The
Black Forest; Or, The Cavern of Horrors" (1802).

The vampire strikes! The frontispiece for "The Bride of the Isles" (*circa* 1820) which is credited to Lord Byron!

VI

THE OLD TOWER OF FRANKENSTEIN

Anonymous

One of the most remarkable finds I made in the 'bluebooks' was the following story, "The Old Tower of Frankenstein", which had originally come from a collection of German ghost stories which Mary Shelley read during that famous summer of 1816 in Switzerland when she was to write her classic horror novel, *Frankenstein; Or, The Modern Prometheus.* The story of how, after reading the book together, Mary, her lover the poet Percy Bysshe Shelley (still engrossing himself in tales of terror!), Lord Byron and John Polidori set each other the challenge of writing a ghost story to relieve the boredom of endless rainy days, and from which resulted *Frankenstein* and Polidori's outstanding story, *The Vampire,* is so well known to enthusiasts of macabre literature that it requires no more than passing mention. That several influences were at work on Mary in the writing of the story—including her companions and the contemporary experiments in galvanism—is indisputable; and indeed she herself admitted that the collection which sparked the group's literary project was also important among these. The book had originated in Germany under the simple title of *Fantasmagoria, circa* 1810, and a year later translated versions were available in both English and French. The stories were ideal material for the 'bluebook' presses, and about 1812, one of the leading publishers, Thomas Tegg, put out a selection of the original also under the title of *Phantasmagoria.* According to Mary Shelley's biographers, the copy of the book which her party read was a French translation, but the contents were virtually identical to those in the English 'bluebook' and both contained "The Old Tower of Frankenstein". Though not a particularly unusual little story, the setting might well have registered with Mary when she had evolved the idea of a scientist endeavouring to create life: in any event, the name of the castle and Mary's chosen name for her central character might seem more than coincidence. The publisher of the English *Phantasmagoria*, Thomas Tegg, of Cheapside, was one of the busiest in the 'Shilling Shocker' trade and rarely missed the opportunity to cash in on available material. Tegg (1776–1848), who called himself a 'Publisher, Re-publisher, Printer and Book-buyer' and was widely known as the 'Lord of the Remainder Trade', had the saving grace of producing some of the best-printed and most attractively illustrated 'bluebooks'—and the distinction of first publishing in English the German story which, in all probability, helped in the creation of the immortal *Frankenstein* . . .

*   *   *

Two LOVERS, a youth and a maiden, once lived on the banks of the Rhine, where it winds between lofty rocks, and is overhung with gloomy forests. The passage-barques go furiously with the stream of the river in this part, and the helmsman used to return thanks when he saw behind him the old Tower of Frankenstein. From this ruin, standing upright and alone, like a pine tree, the owl still sent a long and loud cry, when the shadow of night fell heavily from the lofty bank over the boiling current of the profound water.

In the shadow of this edifice did the couple now stand, hand in hand, when the young man softly spoke:

"Once only do I desire to have thee to myself, without fear of spies, that I may be free to the delight which thy presence brings, did not the eyes of jealous suspicion watch me."

The maiden listened to his pleading breath, and tears filled her light blue eyes; but she spoke not in reply, for her heart beat so fast it held speechless her tongue.

Then at a sound from above, the youth spoke again:

"But look up! Behold the single tower of Frankenstein; hear how the owl brings forth his loud and lonely cry, and the shadow of the tower is cast across the deep water. Say, dearest, dost thou love me? Then let us haste to that tower for when the owl cries, at the safe midnight hour, it will be free to only us."

At these words, the maiden trembled and she came closer to the side of her lover. At last she spoke:

"I dare not meet you at the castle ruins for that foul bird chills my bones with thoughts of the dread curse that hangs o'er it."

And glancing up again, the maiden thinks on the story of the spirit of the woman and her child once sacrificed to the monster and said to haunt the tower though the creature lay slain by the Baron Frankenstein these many years. A chill grips her gentle frame and pale is her cheek.

But the youth, his blood now in passion risen, will not be stilled. Even should the spirits be there, he boldly charges, maybe if they go they can release the unhappy souls as some stories say. He vows that they must meet in the shade of the tower the very next night and pleads anew with his dear love. For a while she is still, then a tremble shakes her body, but she stoutly replies,

"I will, love."

Another day has passed and the moon once more ascended. The breeze came chill and with a swelling noise from the forest, and the hills behind; the voice of the river rose and a melancholy shade fell over the old ruins.

But now what form is that which ascends the rocky pathway towards the grey ruin? It is the maiden that climbs amongst the waving bushes in the steep and narrow track. Her white dress flutters in the air—her steps slide—she pauses as if she would return. Midnight is near—she advances again; and now she is lost in the dark shade of the old ruined tower.

But the dauntless chevalier has met his beloved one, and tears of joy and gratitude run down his flushed cheeks; his arms entwine her waist—they are in the courtyard of the tower—their eyes are full of love. They are seated on the soft moss that springs from the ancient stones. High beats the heart of the youth, for here suspicion does not watch; but the maiden trembles—her hands are cold—she is weak and timid, and mutters as a sick child—a clammy horror creeps over her senses, as she regards the blackness of a low doorway full before her face. It once led to the pit of tears, the deep dungeon of the ancient tower.

In vain rushes through the ruin the power of the storm; in vain howl the gusts of the uprisen tempest through the desolate place.

The angel of female shame is about to fly—when, lo! a burst of rain and thunder—the heavy bird gives a last cry, and strikes, with flapping wing, affrighted from his dark roost. A dead silence prevails, and from the church steeple is heard the midnight hammer of the old bell.

What rises from the black mouth of the fearful dungeon? The eyes of the lovers are fixed as by a supernatural power. Is it fog? Is it cloud? Is it a human shape? A spectral woman comes forth; she advances towards the maiden and the youth; an infant lies at her bosom, half covered by a stained shroud.

Then did the doleful vision speak:

"Now is the doom accomplished, now is the curse lifted," uttered the pale lips of the spectral woman. "The decree is fulfilled, for by your attendance here two souls are this night rescued from the curse under which they were flung those long years ago."

She ceased. The maiden sunk low her head—the lover regarded her with a look of troubled affection. Slowly she raised the shroud-wrapped child. Mercy, mercy! was chanted in the air above: sweet sounds of harps were heard, and all had vanished in a flood of morning splendour.

Soon all had disappeared, and in a calm and lovely morning, with the sun shedding brilliancy upon the waters of the noble Rhine, the guiltless lovers descended from the old castle of Frankenstein.

VII

THE BRIDE OF THE ISLES

A Tale Founded on the Popular Legend of the Vampire

Anonymous

As I mentioned in the previous introduction, the literary gathering in Switzerland in 1816 not only gave the world *Frankenstein*,
but John Polidori's pioneer story of the undead, *The Vampire*—
which, when it was first published in 1819, was attributed to Lord
Byron as a sales gimmick! In any event, the sensation caused by
the story of a man seemingly dead who preserved his existence
by regular intakes of human blood, was instantly taken up by
the worlds of art and literature, and in the years which followed
other stories and plays on the topic proliferated. One of the most
successful of these plays was *The Vampire; Or, The Bride of the
Isles*, which was first presented at the English Opera House in
London in August 1820. This was actually an adaptation of a
French melodrama, *Le Vampire*, which had been prepared for
English audiences by a prolific young playwright, James Robinson
Planché (1796–1880). The original French author had inexplicably
set the play in Scotland, and although Planché rightly insisted to
the theatre proprietor, Samuel Arnold, that vampires were unknown there, he was told that Scottish music and dress had already
been prepared and 'the public will neither know nor care',
according to Arnold. This indeed proved to be the case, for *The
Vampire* was a great success and enjoyed a long run at the theatre.
The production was also notable because a 'Vampire Trap' had
been specially invented for it which enabled the central figure to
disappear in a most sensational manner. During my research into
the 'bluebook' phenomenon, I was fascinated to find that an enterprising publisher, J. Charles of Mary Street, Dublin (of all places!),
had produced a sixpenny adaptation of the play complete with a

dramatic, hand-coloured frontispiece (illustrated elsewhere). He, too, had also taken the liberty of crediting the story to Lord Byron! It was not unusual for the 'Shilling Shockers' to use popular drama as another source of material, but this is certainly one of the best adaptations I have seen, and as it is also a very early vampire story, of considerable interest and importance to all students of the horror genre.

*   *   *

" ' T H O U G H the cheek be pale, and glared the eye, such is the wondrous art the hapless victim blind adores, and drops into their grasp like birds when gazed on by a basilisk."

T H E R E   I S   A popular superstition *still extant* in the southern isles of Scotland, but not with the force as it was a century since, that the souls of persons, whose actions in the mortal state were so wickedly attrocious as to deny all possibility of happiness in that of the next; were doomed to everlasting perdition, but had the power given them by infernal spirits to be for a while the scourge of the living.

This was done by allowing the wicked spirit to enter the body of another person at the moment their own soul had winged its flight from earth; the corpse was thus reanimated—the same look, the same voice, the same expression of countenance, with physical powers to eat and drink, and partake of human enjoyments, but with the most wicked propensities, and in this state they were called vampires. This second existence as it may not improperly be termed, is held on a tenure of the most horrid and diabolical nature. Every *All-Hallow E'en*, he must wed a lovely virgin, and slay her, which done, he is to catch her warm blood and drink it, and from this draught he is renovated for *another* year, and free to take *another* shape, and pursue his Satanic course; but if he failed in procuring a wife at the appointed time, or had not opportunity to make the sacrifice before the moon set, the vampire *was no more*—he did not turn into a skeleton, but literally vanished into air and nothingness.

One of these demoniac sprites, Oscar Montcalm, of infamous notoriety in the Scotch annals of crime and murder (who was decapitated by the hands of the common executioner), was a most successful vampire, and many were the poor unfortunate maidens who had been sacrificed to support his supernatural career, roving from place to place, and every year changing his shape as opportunity presented itself, but always chosing to enter the corpse of some man of rank and power, as by that means his voracious appetite for luxury was gratified.

Oscar Montcalm had seen, and distantly adored in his mortal state, the superior beauty of the Lady Margaret, daughter of the Baron of the Isles, the good Lord Ronald; but, such was his situation, he had not dared to address her; however, he did not forget her in his vampire state, but marked her out for one of his victims, in revenge for the scorn with which he had been treated by her father.

Lady Margaret, though lovely and well proportioned, entered her twentieth year unmarried, nor had she ever been addressed by a suitor whom she could regard with the least partiality, and with much anxiety she sought to know whether she should ever enter into wedlock, and what sort of person her future lord would be. With credulity pardonable to the times in which she lived, and the narrow education then given to females, even of rank, she consulted Sage, Seer and Witch, as to this important event; but it is not to be wondered at that she met with many contradictions, everyone telling a different tale. At length urged on by the irresistible desire to pry into futurity, she repaired with her two maidens, Effie and Constance, to the Cave of Fingal, where, cutting off a lock of her hair, and joining it to a ring from her finger, she cast it into the well, according to the directions she had received from Merna, the Hag of the mountains, who had instructed the fair one as to this expedition.

No sooner was the ring flung into the well than a dreadful storm arose; the torches, which the attendant maidens had borne, were extinguished, and the immense cave was in utter darkness: loud and dreadful was the thunder, accompanied by a horrid confusion of sounds, which beggars description.

Margaret and her companions sunk on their knees; but they were too stupefied with horror to pray, or to endeavour to retrace their way out of this den of horrors. Of a sudden, the cave was brilliantly illuminated, but with no visible means of light, for there were neither torch, lamp, or candle. Solemn music was heard, slow and awfully grand, and in a few minutes two figures appeared, one heavy, morose in countenance, and clad in dark robes, who announced herself as Una, the spirit of the storm, and touching a sable curtain, discovered to the view of Margaret the figure of a noble young warrior, Ruthven, Earl of Marsden, who had accompanied her father to the wars. Again the storm resounded, the curtain closed, and the cave resumed its darkness; but this was only transient—the brilliant light returned—Una was gone, and the light figure, dressed in transparent robes, sprinkled over with spangles remained. With her wand she pulled aside the curtain, and a young man of interesting appearance was visible, but his person was a stranger to the fair one. Ariel, the spirit of the Air, then waved her hand to the entrance of the cave, as a signal for them to depart, and bowing low, they withdrew, amid strains of heart-thrilling harmony, rejoiced to find themselves once more in an open space, and they happily returned in safety to the baron's castle. The Lady Margaret was well pleased with what she had seen, as promising her two husbands, though she was somewhat puzzled by calling to mind a couplet that Ariel had repeated three or four times, while the curtain remained undrawn.

"But once fair maid, will you be wed,
You'll know no second bridal bed."

What could this mean? Surely she would never stoop to illicit desires or intrigue? She thought she knew her own heart too well.

The vampire had seen into the designs of Margaret to visit the Cave of Fingal, and he sought out Ariel and Una, to whom, by virtue of his supernatural rights, he had easy access. The spirit of the air would not befriend him, but the spirit of the storm assisted him to pry into futurity; and to suit his views, she presented the figure of Ruthven, Earl of Marsden. In the meantime, Marsden had the good fortune to save Lord Ronald's life in the battle, and the wars being ended, or at least suspended for a time, he invited the gallant youth home with him to his castle, to pass a few months amid the social rites of hospitality and the pleasure of the chase.

The Lady Margaret received her father with dutiful affection, and gratitude to providence for his safe return, and she beheld young Marsden with secret delight; but when informed that he had preserved the baron from overpowering enemies, her gratitude knew no bounds, and she looked so beautiful and engaging, while returning her thankful effusions for the service he had rendered her father, that the earl could not resist the impulse, and from that hour became deeply enamoured of the lovely fair one.

Marsden's rank and birth were unexceptionable but his fortune was very inadequate to support a title, which made him (added to the love of military glory) enter into the profession of arms, of which he was an ornament.

Margaret was the only child, and her father abounding in wealth and honours; it might therefore be presumed that an ambition might lead him to form very exalted views for the aggrandisement of his heiress; and so he had, but perceiving how high his preserver stood in the good graces of his darling child, and that the passion was becoming mutual, he resolved not to give any interruption to their happiness, but if Marsden could win Margaret to let him have her, as a rich reward for the service he had performed amid the clang of arms.

Parties were daily formed by the baron for the chase, hawking, or fishing, while the evening was given to the festive dance, or the minstrels tuned their harps in the great hall, and sang the deeds of Scottish chiefs, long since departed, amongst whom the heroic Wallace was not forgot.

The love of Ruthven and Lady Margaret were now generally known throughout the islands and congratulations poured in from every quarter.

A day was fixed for the nuptials, and magnificent preparations were made at the castle for the celebration of the ceremony, when the sudden and severe illness of the baron caused a delay. He wished them not to defer their marriage on his account; but the young people, in this instance would not obey him, declaring their joys would be incomplete without his revered presence.

The baron blessed them for this instance of love and filial duty, but he still felt a strong desire to have the marriage concluded.

The baron was scarce recovered, when he and Ruthven were summoned to the field of battle, a war having broken out in Flanders, and the marriage was deferred till their return; and taking a most affectionate leave of the Lady Margaret, the father and lover left the castle, and the fair one in the charge of old Alexander, the faithful steward, with many commands and cautions respecting the edifice and the lady, whom they both regarded as a gem of inestimable value, with whom they were loath to part, but imperious duty and the calls of honour allowed no alternative.

Robert, the old steward's son, attended the baron abroad; and Marsden took his own servant the faithful Gilbert. They were successful in several skirmishes with the enemy, but in the final engagement Ruthven lost his life, dying in the arms of the Lord of the Isles, who mourned over him as for a beloved son, and he ordered Robert and Gilbert, who were on the spot, to convey the body to a place beyond the carnage, that when the battle was over he might see it (if he himself survived) and have the valued remains interred in a manner that became an earl and a soldier, dying in defending his country's cause.

The battle ended, for the glory and success of Great Britain, and the good Baron of the Isles was unhurt, so was Robert, but Gilbert was amongst the slain.

Lord Ronald, fatigued with the sharp action of the day, in which he had borne his part with a vigour surprising to his time of life, for his head was now silvered over with the honourable badge of age, repaired to his tent to take some refreshment and an hour's rest on his couch, to invigorate his frame. The couch eased his weary limbs, but his eyes closed not, and all his thoughts were on Ruthven, and the distress the sad news would give to his dear child. He arose, and with trembling fingers penned a letter to her, describing the melancholy event, and exhorting her, for the sake of her father, to support this trial with resignation and patience, and bow to the dispensations of Providence, who orders all things eventually for the best, however severe and distressing they seem at the time. He ended his letter by observing that he should return to the castle of the Isles without delay, being anxious to fold her in his arms, and that he should bring the corpse of the brave Marsden to his native land.

The letter being sent off expressly by one of his retainers, the baron ordered some soldiers to attend with a bier, and taking Robert for their guide they went to fetch the body of Ruthven, and in the meantime he had a small tent erected for its reception, surmounted by a sable flag.

But this posthumous attention of the good baron was all in vain, for after a long absence, Robert and the soldiers returned, with the unwelcome news that the body of the gallant Scot was not to be found, but the spot where it had been deposited by the servants was still marked with the blood that had flowed from his gaping wounds and it was presumed that the enemy had found the corpse, and had conveyed it away to some obscure hole out of revenge for the slaughter he had dealt among their leaders before his fall. This event added materially to Ronald's regret and sorrow, for the natives of the Isles of Escotia held a traditional superstition, that while the body lay unburied the spirit wandered denied of rest. He offered rewards for the body without success, and was at length obliged, though with much reluctance, to drop the affair.

The baron was obliged to pay his duty in England to his sovereign before he repaired to the Isles. Unexpected events detained him two months at the British court, but he at last effected his departure to his long wished-for home.

A courier made known his approach, and Lady Margaret, attended by the whole household, dressed in their best array, came forth to meet him, headed by the aged minstrel, and they received their lord with joyous shouts and lively strains, about half a mile from the gates of the castle.

Lord Ronald, as the carriage descended a steep hill that led into the valley, had a full view of the party approaching to meet him, and his heart felt elated at the compliment. He could discern his daughter; but how came it she was not in sables? Surely Ruthven, her betrothed lover, deserved that mark of respect to his memory! But he could observe that she was gaily dressed, and her high plume of feathers waving in the light breeze that adulated the air. The baron cast a look on his own deep mourning, and sighed; he was not pleased—but worse and worse. As he gained a nearer view, he perceived that his daughter was handed along, most familiarly by a knight. I had hoped, said he to himself, that Margaret would have rose superior to the inconstancy and caprice attributed to her sex. Can it be possible, that she has so soon forgot the valiant, accomplished Ruthven! Oh, woman! woman! are ye all alike? As the vehicle entered the valley, Ronald quitted it, to receive the welcome of his child and retainers.

Powers of astonishment! Was it, or was it not, illusion? By what miracle did he behold Ruthven, Earl of Marsden, standing before him, and Lady Margaret hanging with chaste expressions of delight on his arm; there was a scar on his forehead, and he was much paler than before the battle, but no other alteration was visible. As for Robert, he stood aghast, his hair bristled up and his joints trembled, and altogether would have served as a good model of horror to a painter or statuary.

Ruthven stretched forth his hand—"You seem astonished, my good lord," said he, "to find me here before you, or, indeed to find me here at all. I was discovered by some peasants returning from their daily labour, nearly covered with fern and leaves ["Yes," said Robert, "that was Gilbert's work and mine."] by means of a little dog, who had scented out my body from its purposed concealment. They were very poor, and my clothes and decorations were a strong temptation, to which they yielded, they agreed to strip me, sell the clothes, and divide the spoil. While they were thus occupied, they perceived signs of life, and their humanity prevailed over every other consideration, I was conveyed to one of their cottages, and well attended. The man had a wonderful skill in herbs and simples, therefore my cure was rapid, but previous to my leaving them, I well rewarded everyone who had been instrumental in my preservation and freely forgave the intended plunder they had confessed to me, as it was the means directed by fate to prolong my existence, and restore me to my angelic Margaret.

"When I recovered, I found the British forces had quitted Flanders, but I could not learn which direction my friend the baron (you my dear lord) had taken; so I hastened to Scotland with all the speed my situation would admit of, and we were retarded at sea by adverse winds. I found my dear betrothed, and her fair damsels, in deep mourning for my supposed loss; but I soon changed her tears for smiles, and her sables for gayer vestments: but at first her surprise, like yours, Lord Ronald, was too great to admit of utterance, but in time we became composed and grateful, and we agreed not to inform you of my existence, but astonish you on your arrival."

The baron greeted his young friend most warmly and testified his hope that no more ill-omened events would disappoint the nuptials of the brave earl and Margaret, whom he tenderly clasped to his bosom, and kissing each cheek, remarked that she was the living image of his dear departed wife. He then turned to the old harper, and bidding him strike up a lively strain, proceeded to the castle, where all was joy and festivity; again resounded the song, and again the damsels, with their swains showed off their best reels *à la Caledonia.*

In the old steward's room a plenteous board was spread, for the upper servants and retainers of the hospitable Lord of the Isles, who ordered flowing bowls and well replenished horns to the health of Ruthven and Margaret.

Some of the party were remarking on the wonderful preservation of Marsden's earl by the Flemish peasants, instead of plundering and leaving him to perish, as many would have done to an almost expiring enemy.

"*Almost expiring!*" said Robert, whose cheeks had not yet recovered their usual hue since the meeting in the valley with Ruthven.

"*Almost expiring!*" he repeated; "I am certain the body of the earl was dead—aye, as dead as my great grandsire—when I and Gilbert carried him from the field of battle; and when we left him under the fern he was as cold as ice, and the blood from his wounds coagulated—No, no, he never came to life again; this Ruthven you have here must be a vampire."

"*A vampire! a vampire!*" resounded from all the company, with loud shouts of laughter at poor Robert's simplicity. "Perhaps you are a *vampire*," said his sweetheart, Effie, joining in the mirth, "so I shall take care how I trust myself in your power."

Robert did not reply, and all the rest of the night he had to stand the bantering jests of his companions.

But Robert was right; Marsden's earl died on the field of battle, and the moment the servants quitted the corpse, the vampire, wicked Montcalm, whose relics lay mouldering beneath a stone in Fingal's cave, watching the moment, took possession, and re-animated the body; the wounds instantly healed, but the face wore a pallid hue, the invariable case with the vampires, their blood not flowing in that free circulation which belongs to real mortals.

The story told by the vampire was a fabrication, respecting the peasants, to impose on Lord Ronald and the Lady Margaret as to the appearance of the supposed Ruthven, and he well succeeded.

On previously consulting the Spirit of the Storm, the vampire had discovered that Margaret would be courted by Ruthven, Earl of Marsden; he also discovered, in his peep into futurity, that the young hero would be slain in battle, and this seemed to him a glorious opportunity to obtain possession of the lovely Margaret, and make her his victim, renovate his vampireship, and go on in the most diabolical career, hurling destruction on the human race, and drawing them into crime after crime, till they sank into the gulph of eternal infamy.

It now wanted a month to All-Hallow E'en and it so chanced, that in that year the next coming moon would set on that very eve from its full orbit. The vampire repaired to the cave of Fingal, and by magic means, which he well knew how to put in execution, he raised up some infernal spirits, whom he asked for orders. They told him they would consult their ruler Beelzebub, and he was to come on the third eve from thence for an answer.

This, then, was the decree—he must wed a virgin, destroy her, and drink her blood, before the setting of the moon on All-Hallow E'en, or terminate into mere nonentity; and if the maid was unchaste, the charm was dissolved. If he succeeded he was to quit the form of Earl Marsden and get egress into some other corpse to give it animation.

The supposed death of Ruthven had caused Margaret to imbibe the idea that the two figures she had seen in Fingal's cave, and Ariel's couplet prophetic but of one marriage, now made out by his fall, he being only a betrothed lover, and the stranger knight she regarded as her future spouse; but the return of the Earl again puzzled her, and she knew not what to think, but at length resolved on another visit to the mystic cavern. Possibly ashamed of confessing this weakness to her maidens, or, what is more probable, conscious that from the terrors they had experienced in attending her there, she could not persuade them to go a second time, she went alone, and soon after midnight, when all the castle was hushed in sound repose, save the vampire, who beheld from the lofty casement, the temporary flight of the enterprising Margaret. How did he thirst for her blood—how willingly would he have immolated the lovely maid that moment, and paid the infernal tribute, but for one clause that interposed and saved her from his fangs. This was the necessity of his being first legally married, in all due form, to the intended victim. He regarded her with a diabolical and malicious scowl, while, by as bright a starlight night as ever illumined the heavens, he saw her tripping through the park's wide avenues of stately firs. He wondered where she was going, and felt apprehensive that some event was in agitation that might deprive him of his bride. The vampire had just concluded to follow her, when a heaviness he could neither resist or shake off, overpowered him and sealed his eyes in a deep sleep.

Margaret, in much perturbation and a beating heart, gained the way to the cave; but the interior was so dark that she was obliged to grope on her hands and knees to the magic well, and cast in the accustomed charm. The thunder rolled, and the storm commenced, but with not one quarter of the violence as on her preceding visit. The music followed in an harmonious strain, and the spirits of the storm and air soon stood before her. The beauty, the innocence, of the noble maid, her virtues and her benevolence, had interested these mystical beings in her behalf—yes, even the stern and oft obdurate Una felt for Margaret, and wished to save her. They could not alter the decree of fate, nor had they power over the vampires; the only thing that remained was to warn the enquirer, if possible, of her danger. For this purpose, they unfolded the curtain, and presented to her view, the real Ruthven on the field of battle, bleeding and a corpse. She heard his last sigh, saw his last convulsive motion—*a grizzly fleshless skeleton stood by his side, and at that moment entered his corpse, which sprung up reanimated*! Margaret knew well the traditional tales of the vampires, and shuddered as she beheld one before her; for what could be more plain? No further vision was shown her—she was warned from the cave, and the fair one returned to the castle, dejected and spiritless. What did this mean? Ruthven, her adored Ruthven, could be no vampire—impossible—so accomplished, so clever, superior in most things to others of his rank. She passed the intervening hours in a very restless state, till they met at their morning repast in the small saloon. The vampire handed her to a chair; she remembered the scene in the cave, and shrank back with a feeling of disgust; but this was not lasting; the labours of the spirit of the storm and the air had not their intended effect; like advice given to young maidens that accords not with the inclination, it sank before the fascination of the object beloved, and she regarded what had been shown her as wayward spite in Una and Ariel; so ready are we to twist circumstances to act in conformity with our own inclination.

The dews of night, the chilling breeze, the damp of the magic cave of Fingal, joined to the fatigue and agitation of the noble maiden, caused a fever which confined her to her chamber several days, and again delayed the marriage. The vampire grew impatient, and before the Lady Margaret was scarce convalescent, he began to press for the nuptial ceremony, with what the good baron thought indecorous haste, though he made all possible allowance for repeated disappointments and youthful passions.

Robert, much better read than the warrior, his master, in the traditional tales of his country, and its populuar superstitions, had not yet got the better of his shock at the reappearance of Ruthven in his native valley, when he felt convinced that Marsden's earl died of his wounds on the field of battle at Flanders. "Aye, by the holy rood, he did," would the youth often mutter to himself. "May I never live to be married to my gentle Effie, and it wants but three days and three nights to that happy morn, if I did not see Ruthven's eye-strings crack, and his heart's veins burst assunder: this is a vampire, and this is the moon when those foul fiends pay their tribute, and now he is all impatience to wed my young mistress, forsooth—Yes, yes, 'tis plain enough: but what is the use of saying anything about it, my father and all the servants laugh at me; even my intended turns into ridicule, anything I advance on the subject, and calls me Robert, the vampire hunter: but I will not be deterred from doing my duty like an honest servant, let them jeer as they will. I am resolved to tell the baron all that I know, that is, all I think of his guest, and then he may please himself, and come what will, my conscience will be clear."

Robert had courage to face a cannon, and never turned his back on the bravest foe, but he felt daunted at the disclosure he meant to make to Lord Ronald; the subject was awkward, and the vampire (if vampire he was) might take a summary revenge on him for his interference. Yet his resolution was not shaken, and seeking the cellar-man he procured a glass of cordial and a horn of ale to revive his spirits, and then, finding himself what he called his own man again, he sought the baron, whom he happened to find alone and taking his evening walk in the grounds, while Margaret and her lover were sitting at their music.

Robert told his tale with much hesitation and faltering, but the baron heard him with more patience than he expected, and made him recount every particular of his suspicions. "'Tis strange! 'tis marvellous strange!" replied the good Lord Ronald; "for I have seen many persons from Flanders, and yet they never heard of the Earl of Marsden being saved by the peasants: one would have thought such news would have spread like wildfire."

"Neither does he go to mass or prayer," observed Robert, "as a Christian warrior ought to do; nor does he take salt on his trencher.* And All-Hallow E'en is fast approaching," continued Robert: "this is the fatal moon, and my young mistress—"

"Shall never be his," exclaimed the baron, " 'till the moon sets, and the night, so tragic and pregnant of evil to many a spotless maid, is gone by; then if Ruthven is Marsden's true earl, he may have my Margaret. She shall then be his, and I will turn all my fish ponds into bowls for whisky punch, and the great fountain in the forecourt shall flow with ale till not a Scot around can stand upon his legs, or he is no well-wisher to me or mine; but if he is an infernal vampire, his reign will be over. Faith, by St Andrew, I know not what to think, but I have had fearful dreams, portentous of evil to my ancient house."

The baron dismissed Robert with a present, and many encomiums on his fidelity and zeal for him and the Lady Margaret. "My father," said the honest fellow, "has lived with you from youth to age: I was born within these walls, and my deceased mother suckled your amiable heiress; treachery in me would be double guilt: no, I would die to serve the house of Ronald!"

When the baron entered his daughter's apartment, a group met his eyes, very ill calculated to give him pleasure in his present frame of mind full of supernatural ideas, and teeming with dread suspicions; Margaret had changed her robes of plaid silk for virgin white, her neck chain, bracelets and other ornaments of filigree silver, most exquisitely wrought. Ruthven was also dressed

* This remark of Robert's was another popular superstition of the Isles.

with elegance. The fair one's attendants were also in their best. The steward and the physician of the household were present, and the chaplain stood with the sacred book in his hand.

"We were waiting for you, my dear Lord Baron," said the vampire, Ruthven; "I have persuaded my lovely betrothed to be mine this very evening. We have been so very unfortunate, that I dread further delay, and think every hour teeming with evil till she is mine irrevocably."

"You have no rival," answered the baron, much alarmed and piqued: "you are secure in Margaret's love and my consent. My friends and tenants will ill brook such privacy; they have been accustomed to see the daughters of the Lord of the Isles wedded in public pomp and magnificence, and to share in the festive and abundant hospitalities. No, by the shades of my ancestors, I will have no such doings."

Ruthven pleaded hard, but the baron heeded not his arguments or eloquence, for the more he seemed bent on espousing Margaret then, the old lord thought more on Robert's report and his own suspicions. Margaret, infatuated by the spell that cast an illusion over her senses, seemed to forget her proper dignity and the delicate decorum of her sex, and joined in the solicitations of her lover. "My dear father," said the beauteous maiden, "Ruthven and myself are in unison with each other's sentiments; we seek not in pomp and glare for happiness; we place our prospects of future bliss in elegant retirement and domestic pleasures. Allow us to be now united, I entreat you, and you can afterwards treat your neighbours, retainers, and servants, as plenteously as you like, but I shrink from the idea of a public marriage."

Ruthven took the hand of his betrothed, which she presented to him with the most endearing smiles, while her eyes modestly bent down and her cheeks covered with roseate blushes, and never did Lady Margaret look so irresistibly captivating as at that moment.

The baron, while she was speaking, trembled with emotion— Not for a single hour, said he, mentally, would I defer their happiness on account of bridal pomp, if I thought all was right; but I will not risk the sacrificing of so much loveliness, and that my only child, the image of my lost Cassandra, to a vampire; but he did not like to disclose the suspicions he had imbibed, for if they were founded in error, how grossly ridiculous would he appear, and he resolved to delay the nuptials, and stay the test of the moon. He therefore said, "It is my pleasure to give a full month to splendid preparation, 'tis but a short delay, and let me have the satisfaction to have the nuptials as I would wish them to be, in honour of Marsden's earl and Ronald's daughter."

The baron observed the lover give a start at the words 'a full month', and his eyes shot forth a most malicious glance. He still held Margaret's hand. "Nonsense! my good friend," said he, "this is not fair, from one warrior to another—Chaplain, begin the ceremony."

The enraged baron flung off his guard, snatched the book from the hands of the priest, and bade Margaret retire with her maidens to another room, accusing Ruthven of being a vampire.

This was strongly resented by the accused, and, indeed, every one took his part, and laughed at the suggestion. This raised the baron's passion so high that he was declared by the physician to be insane, and they coercively conveyed him to his chamber, and barred him in, where he was on the point of becoming frantic indeed, from the thoughts of his injunctions, for he was more convinced than ever of Ruthven being a supernatural imposter, or he would never have acted so uncourteous to a knight in his own castle.

Robert having heard from his father, the old steward, of the interruption of the marriage through the baron's mania, in thinking the Earl of Marsden a vampire, and his lord's confinement in the western turret, observed that he supposed the nuptials then were all off. His parent answered no, that the young people were not forced to obey such whims; that Lady Margaret was retired for an hour to regain her composure, and the chaplain would then perform the ceremony. "And who is to be the bride's father?" said Robert.—"I am to have that honour," replied the steward.— "And much good may it do you," said the son: "but if I was you, I'd cater better for the noble Lady Margaret than to give her to an evil spirit."—"Go to, for an ungracious bird," exclaimed Alexander; "you are as mad as your master; poor Effie will have but a crazy husband at the best of it."—"Better a crazy one, than a bloodthirsty vampire, father," observed Robert, who quitted the room, vexed at the loud peal of laughter, which was now set up against him.

Robert went out into the park, but returned privately into the castle by a bypath and a private door, of which he had a key, having procured it some time before he went to the wars, for he was then a rakish youth, and loved to steal out to the village dance or festival, after he was supposed to retire to rest for the night; but now he was contracted to the languishing blue-eyed Effie he was reformed, and voluntarily relinquished all such stolen delights. The key was now regarded by him as a treasure. "It helped me," said he to himself, "to sow my wild oats; it shall now aid me to perform a more laudable purpose. Little did I think to see the good Baron of the Isles a captive in his own castle; and for what, but that he is in too much possession of his senses to sacrifice his lovely virgin daughter to a vampire, for such, by the holy rood, is this fine Earl of Marsden. Why his face is the image of death itself, and his eyes glare; yet my Lady Margaret forsooth! thinks him very handsome, now she is under the influence of the wicked spell; the real Ruthven looked not so when he came to woo the noble fair one; but he says 'tis through his wounds in battle: I think by St Cuthbert, he has had time enough to get his complexion again, and he eats and drinks voraciously, it makes me sick to see him as I stand in waiting, and no salt—faugh!"

This long soliloquy brought the faithful youth to the door of the baron's prison; he drew the bolts and entered; his lord was pacing the chamber with unmeasured strides, and beating his forehead, while heavy sighs burst from his aged bosom. He started and stood still on Robert's entrance.

"Friend or foe?" said he.—"Friend," replied Robert, "and when I prove otherwise to my most noble master and commander, may I be seized by the foul fiend and made food for vulture."

"I am not mad," said the good old veteran, "but I think I may say, I am distracted with grief." "You are no more mad than I, my lord; I do not join in that absurd tale; but hasten and arm yourself. The marriage is to take place almost immediately—let us hasten and prevent it, ere it is too late."

Lord Ronald was doubly shocked—his suspicions of the vampire were increased by this obstinate persisting in the nuptials against his command, and the want of tenderness and filial love testified by his daughter. How changed was Margaret! Did she choose for her bridal hours those of confinement to her sire—had she not supposed him insane, it is not to be thought she would have suffered him to be thus treated; this then was her season for connubial joys—the sudden insanity of her only surviving parent, he who had so ardently strove not only to fulfil his own duties, but to supply the place as far as possible of the late Lady Cassandra, his amiable wife, and he felt there was no sting so keen as a child's ingratitude. The barbed arrow seemed to touch his very vitals, and for the first time in his life the brave Ronald shed tears.

"Take courage, my lord," said Robert, "if they dare still to oppose your authority, this trusty falchion, this well-tried steel, shall prove if Ruthven is common flesh and blood or no."

"Moderation! moderation! Robert." replied the baron, as he led the way to Lady Margaret's apartment, where he did not arrive one minute too soon—the ceremony was on the point of commencing, and 'tis possible a few of the first words had been pronounced by the priest.

The baron's entrance caused a universal consternation—the maidens shrieked, and the vampire began to bluster, but Lord Ronald took prompt measures. He solemnly protested that he was in the full use and exercise of his senses, and charged his daughter, on the penalty of incurring his curse, not to enter into wedlock with Marsden's earl till he sanctioned it. She did not choose to disobey on such an awful threat, but casting a look of anguish and tenderness on her lover, she burst into tears, and leaning on the arms of her sympathising maidens, withdrew to her chamber, where throwing herself on a couch, gave way to a full tide of sorrow. "Cruel father!" she exclaimed. "Ridiculous superstition! I feel I never shall be the bride of my truly adored and adoring Ruthven, so many fatal interruptions seem as if the fates forbid our union—spirits of the storm and air, are ye not too in league against me?"

The vampire now besought the baron's forgiveness and friendship, attributing his recent behaviour to excess of love, that did not brook delay; he also interceded for the chaplain, whom Lord Ronald was about to dismiss for his presumption, and peace was again restored in the Castle of the Isles.

Wine was called for, and a repast was spread and the vampire so artfully strove against the suspicions of the baron, that the prejudices of the latter were nearly done away; and Robert blamed for his credulous folly; yet the false earl could not obtain from the old nobleman a promise to allow him to wed before the setting of the moon, for Ronald still adhered to that test, nor would abridge aught of a term that now waxed very short.

The vampire concealed his chagrin and feigned content; he thought it best to keep a firm footing in the castle, as some chance might still operate in his favour, founding his hopes on the spell he had obtained over Lady Margaret, and the strong affection with which she beheld him, and he scarcely admitted a doubt of success, if he could get the baron and Robert out of the way; for no one else in the castle had the least doubt of his being the real Earl of Marsden.

The baron, however, watched with great vigilance, and Robert never stirred from a station he had taken that commanded a view of the door of Lady Margaret's chamber. Time seemed to ride on swift pinions with the vampire—his fears were stronger than his hopes—he had never been so foiled before in his attempts, and he thought it best to provide against the coming danger, and leave the mistress alone for her maid the blue eyed Effie; whom he would lure from her allegiance to Robert, persuade her to wed himself, and then sacrifice her to pay his annual demoniac tribute. This would serve two purposes, renew his vampireship, and be a deadly revenge on the interfering Robert, on whom he longed to wreak his diabolical rage.

It seemed rather a difficult achievement to gain the affections of a young and certainly most virtuous maiden (who was to be married in a few hours to the object of her first choice) from that object, but the vampire's case grew desperate, and he resolved to try if the charm would operate.

While Robert was watching the lady, the vampire resolved to seize on the more ignoble prize, and he assailed Effie with every alluring temptation. He told the poor girl that he was tired of pursuing the match with Lady Margaret, and abhorred the thoughts of allying himself to such a piece of dotage as the credulous baron, who was grown superannuated, and only fit to sit amongst the old wives a-spinning, and tell legendary tales of hobgoblins, and water sprites. He said Effie's beauty and innocence had charmed him—

that she wanted nothing but dress and rank to be level with her mistress, and that would be hers by marrying Marsden's earl.

"But I am ignorant, and can neither play music, sing, dance, or do the honours of a table, like Lady Margaret." This reply pleased the vampire; it seemed one of a very yielding nature, if she had no scruples but what arose from a fear of her own demerits.

"All these can soon be taught," said the deceiver. "I must seek some lady of fallen fortune, but elegant accomplishment, to polish your native gracefulness; she shall be your companion in my absence, and your tutoress, and I will join in the delightful task; therefore that can be no objection." Effie raised several other difficulties, but all were successfully combated, and the vampire earl promised to make the foresaken Robert amends for the loss of his bride by a noble sum and a pretty damsel from off his own estate.

Effie yielded; and though by this act she justly incurred censure and reproach, yet we must do her the justice to remember, that the vampire had a tongue to charm his victims, and eyes that are described like the fascination of a basilisk; and to have a powerful earl sighing for her love, might have tempted a higher maid than the simple Effie, the mere child of nature.

Having gained her consent, he hastened to secure his prize; he persuaded her that they must instantly flee, lest the lynx-eyed Robert should grow jealous, and interrupt their promised happiness; he therefore told her to meet him in an hour, at the end of the long avenue in the castle park, and he would be prepared with a horse to convey her to the next convent (about five miles distant) where the priest could join their hands.

That he intended to wed Effie was too true; in that promise lurked no deceit, but the ceremony over, he meant to take her into an adjacent wood, offer up his sacrifice by immolating her with his own hands, and drinking her heart's blood; then seek out some noble form just departed—enter it—and woo Lady Margaret in a new character, and finally triumph over the baron, for he hated all who opposed him in his designs.

Poor unsuspecting Effie, thy head ran on nothing but the glare of thy expected coronet, and thou felt no pity for thy so lately loved Robert, or thy kind and generous mistress, though both were to be betrayed by this clandestine step.

She was true to her appointment and crossed the park with light steps—the vampire was in waiting—he assisted her to mount the horse, and then sprung up behind her.—The steed bounded off like lightning. In an instant Robert rushed from a copse and cried out for the fugitives to stop, but instead of obeying him the vampire spurred his horse to quicken him on. The baron had taken Robert's post to watch the Lady Margaret while the latter made an excursion for air; his gun was loaded, and vengeance nerved the young soldier's arm with so sure an aim that the corporeal part of the vampire fell mortally wounded to the ground, dragging Effie after it loudly shrieking, and all her new-raised love extinguished —for the illusion had vanished, and the image of Robert again filled her virgin heart. Most happily for her future peace the secret of her consenting to the supposed earl's passion was known to her alone—there had been no witness of that degrading incident so fatal to her integrity; and Robert believing she was carried off against her will, all ended well—she was espoused to her faithful suitor at the appointed time, and made an excellent wife; for her dereliction had made her watchful over herself—she often thought of the precipice on which she had stood and trembled. Her beauty long after her marriage gained her admirers, but they were soon dismissed with spirit, and taught to keep at a proper distance, for Effie was now proof against seduction.

But to return to the vampire. He lay bleeding on the ground, while Robert conveyed Effie to the castle, cautioning her to secrecy as she valued his life, for he knew not what might be the result of this act, if it was indeed Marsden's earl he had slain. He sought the baron who was much vexed at the recital, though he acknowledged that Robert had much provocation, and Ruthven's elopement with Effie was an insult on the Lady Margaret not to be borne. The Lord of the Isles and his faithful follower repaired to the spot where the latter had left the treacherous earl.

"I wonder," said Robert, as they proceeded thither, and calling to mind the scene in Flanders, "whether we shall find his lordship there, or whether Beelzebub has given him a second lift." The vampire, however, was there, bleeding copiously, but in full possession of his senses. He declared life to be ebbing fast, and that he forgave Robert his death wound; also, he ascribed his carrying off Effie as a mere frolic to alarm her and that he had intended to convey her back in safety to the castle. "I do not like such jests," said the indignant Robert, "and you have paid for an act you had better have left alone."

The false earl then proceeded to state, on the oath of a dying man, that he was no vampire. This gave a sad pang both to the baron and Robert, and the former testified his regret at the conduct such suspicions had given rise to. He then demanded of Ruthven if he had any commission to charge him with, and it should be punctually executed.

"Swear it," exclaimed the vampire, eagerly.

The baron drew forth his sword and swore on it.

"Give me that topaz ring from off your finger," said the vampire; "let me die with it on, in token of your renewed amity, and allow it to be buried with me." To this the Lord Ronald most readily consented.

"Next," said the vampire, drawing it forth from his bosom, where it hung extended by a hair chain, "take this ring of twisted gold, and cast it into a well that stands on the north side of Fingal's cave—'tis a charm given by the mighty Stuffa. I shall thus have a vow performed that will give peace to my soul, and save it from wandering after it has quitted its mortal clay-built tenement. In a few minutes I shall be no more—draw my body aside into the copse, and tomorrow at your return you can seek it, and give me burial; but for the present conceal my death from all you meet: name it not until the ring is in the cave."

In a few minutes the vampire seemed to die with a heavy groan, and the afflicted baron and his attendant proceeded to obey the last injunctions thus received, both conscience-stricken at having thus treated Marsden's earl, and feeling assured, from the manner of his death, that he was a mortal man. They returned to the castle to prepare for their journey to the cave; but mentioned not the decease of Ruthven; and even Effie was imposed on to believe that the wounds, though they had bled much, were but trifling. This gave much comfort to the damsel, as it cleared her Robert of a deed of blood.

The baron and Robert set out as soon as it dawned, for the cave of Fingal, to perform what they thought an imperious duty, for as such they considered a posthumous request made under such distressing circumstances.

Little did the credulous pair suspect that they were now made the agents of the wicked vampire, for this is the true story of the magic ring.

The outer part of the vampire was not subject to disease, and it was invincible to the sword. If they could contrive to have Stuffa's ring flung into the well of the cave of Fingal within twenty-four hours after the death wound it was restored to its vile career for the appointed time, and for that season the malignant spirit hovered round the body.

The good Lord of the Isles and Robert arrived safe there, and with little difficulty found the well, for report had spread its situation far and wide owing to its magic qualities. Lord Ronald cast in the ring—instantaneously a hissing, as if of snakes, followed, but soon all was silent as the grave.

They left the cavern and found themselves in the midst of a pelting storm, and their horses, which they had left tied to a tree, were unloosened and they sought in vain for them. As they continued their search a sweet musical voice was heard by the wanderers.

> " 'Tis Ariel bids you haste away,
> 'Tis Ariel warns you not to stay;
> Hie and stop a horrid scene,
> 'Tis the fatal *Hallow E'en*,
> Haste and save the destin'd fair
> From the treacherous vampire's snare!"

"Robert," said the Baron, "did you hear ought or do my ears deceive me?"—again was the verse repeated with this additional stanza—

> "Lose not time but quickly see
> Whose the triumph is to be,
> Margaret must be no more,
> Or the vampire's reign is o'er"

"Tis plain enough, my lord; Ariel, who is always reckoned a benign spirit, warns us.—We are deceived.—Oh this cursed vampire! I see it now, he made us tools for his own purpose."

"Nonsense, my good fellow," said the baron, "it must be some new plot against my peace—a real vampire, for we left Marsden's Earl quite dead."

"Oh, he was dead enough in Flanders," observed Robert, "but he seems to have as many lives as the Witch of Endor's tabby cat. My mind forbodes horrid things.—No harm, however, in getting home quick."

But they were involved in the intricacies of the forest, and it required both patience and perseverance to find the right track; at length they succeeded, and walked on with rapid strides, for the evening wore away. At this juncture some horsemen overtook them.—It was quite dusk and objects scarce discernible.

"Hoy, holla, my good foresters! can you put us in the way for Baron Ronald's castle; the Lord of the Isles we mean," said the foremost of the cavaliers.

"What want you there?" replied the baron (himself), "let us know ere we guide you, for we are going thither."

"I am Hildebrand, Lord Gowen's sister's son, sent by my mother to pay my respects and duty to him as becomes a nephew and a godson, nor has he seen me since my infancy."

"Welcome! Welcome!" exclaimed the baron, "son of my beloved Ellen, I am thy uncle, but by some strange accidents, here on foot with one single follower."

" 'Tis lucky," replied the youth, springing from his steed and embracing the baron, "that we have some led horses in our train." Lord Ronald and Robert were glad to hear of this seasonable supply, and mounting the noble beasts, set off at full speed.

Hildebrand, as they rode along, was made acquainted with recent events by his worthy uncle—he was struck with terror, and felt much interested for the Lady Margaret; for young Gowan had imbibed from the countess (his mother) a strong belief of the existence of vampires, and he intimated, though respectfully, to his venerable uncle, that he had done wrong by throwing the ring into the well, as by that means it was most probable, the wicked sprite had acquired reanimation.

Again the storm arose and served to retard their progress, for the steeds affrighted at the vivid and incessant lightning, could with difficulty be got forward. At length they arrived at the copse, and Robert with two of Earl Gowen's serving men dismounted to seek for the body, but it was not there. "Just as I thought to find it," said the former. "Beshrew me it is an industrious sprite; but the moon will soon set," and as the benign Ariel sang—

> "Let's haste and save the destin'd fair
> From the treacherous vampire's snare."

They spurred their horses, and the storm having made a temporary stop they were soon across the park. Music was sounding—they could distinguish the harper's strain—the great hall was lighted up most brilliantly—a sumptuous altar had been erected at one end —and for the third time, the marriage ceremony was about to begin, when the baron, Lord Gowen and Robert rushed in and secured the intended bride, who fainted immediately, for in the person of her noble cousin she beheld the form shown her by Una and Ariel in the cave of Fingal, and the vampire's charm vanished away like snow before the meridian sun.

The vampire seemed armed with supernatural strength—he resisted all their efforts to subdue him—and their swords made no impression—he struggled hard to bear away the Lady Margaret from the midst of her protectors, and the amazing efforts of the vampire spread horror and alarm, for that he was an evil sprite no one now doubted. He had returned to the castle that evening, and said he came with the baron's consent (who had undertaken a sudden journey) to wed the Lady Margaret, and had brought her father's ring as a token. All was now bustle, preparation and joy, till the unexpected entrance of the Lord of the Isles and his companions, and had it not been for the providence of Gowen seeking the castle that night, the fiend would have triumphed, for they could not have got home on foot in time enough to save her.

But the fiend was not to be overpowered—he jumped on the temporary altar, sword in hand (after having wounded and bit with his teeth several of the domestics), insisting he would yet have his bride. In an instant the scene changed—the moon set—the thunder rolled over the castle, and the bolt fell on the vampire—he rolled lifeless upon the floor, and after a terrific yell, melted into air, incorporeal and invisible to every eye. Thus ended the wicked sprite.

Some months after this event Margaret was happily united to Earl Gowen, with whom she led a happy life till they both sunk into the grave, venerable with age, making good the prediction of the spirits of the cave of Fingal—

"Ne'er but once was she to wed,
Or have a second bridal bed."

VIII

THE LUNATIC AND HIS TURKEY
A Tale of Witchcraft
Anonymous

'Bluebooks' similar to those in Britain were also published in America, although on a rather limited scale, but having had the opportunity to examine some of these items in the New York Public Library, I am glad to be able to include an item from one of them here, "The Lunatic and his Turkey". The volume from which it is taken is entitled *Tales of Witchcraft*, and was published *circa* 1802 by J. Harrison at Yorick's Head, New York. The publication runs to 36 pages and contains a series of stories, most with witchcraft themes, and several based on events at the famous American 'witch village' of Salem. The stories are all surprisingly objective for their period, and "The Lunatic and his Turkey" impressed me by its sceptical tone, not to mention its unusual angle on the witchcraft fears which for so long beset rural communities on both sides of the Atlantic. J. Harrison appears to have published quite a number of 'bluebooks' of this kind, some of which were sold in England (just as certain British publications found their way to America); among the most successful was "Fatal Effects of Jealousy" which the author described as a Spanish novel "Founded on Facts".

*   *   *

THE SINGULAR SUPERSTITION still exists, in some parts of the country, of ascribing those terrible affections of the mind which we see in all the forms of insanity, to the agency of witchcraft. More than one instance has come to the knowledge of the writer, where the inmates of the family afflicted appeared most devoutly to believe that their sick friend was actually bewitched by some foul and malignant demon of the air. Experiments have been tried to detect the malicious hag who haunted the bedside of the suffering patient. Sentries have been set over his chamber, and silent watches kept in 'the witching hour of night', in the hope of intercepting the stealthy visits of the witch—

> Who chooseth solitarie to abide
> Far from all neighbours, that her devilish deedes,
> And hellish arts from people she might hide,
> And hurt far off, unknowne, whomever she envyde.

When these experiments failed, and we have yet to hear of the first that has been successful, others equally profound and philosophical have been resorted to. The blood taken from the arm of the patient by his physician has been covertly placed in some secret closet upon the topmost shelf, to dry away, under the belief that the health of the old witch would from that hour begin to fail, and that she would infallibly die, the moment the process of evaporation ceased. Another mode of operation has been to open the ashes upon the old-fashioned hearth, and pour in the sick man's blood, some expert dame standing ready, with heated shovel, to stir up the embers, under the belief that the witch, whoever or whatever she might be, would get a terrible scorching by the operation.

A singular instance of this species of credulity occurred a few years since in the town of D——. A labouring man, the father of a family in humble circumstances, was attacked with a slight disease, which, after several weeks of illness, terminated in a fixed insanity. The patient was quite harmless and inoffensive, but singular in all his proceedings, and generally wild and incoherent in his conversation. The family, one after another, from certain strange noises they had observed, and the mysterious conversations which they imagined the lunatic to hold with some invisible being, came to the conclusion that he was actually bewitched. All the minor remedies for witchcraft were speedily resorted to. Horseshoes were nailed over every door in the house, and nails, in the form of the cross, driven into the thresholds. Pins were plentifully stuck into the crevices of the windows, and the shovel and tongs carefully placed crosswise upon the hearthstone at the raking up of the fire. But all to no purpose. The sick man was still a lunatic, and no clue could be obtained to his supposed tormentors.

Affairs remained in this situation for several weeks; one friend and another friend advising to this experiment and to that, as their imagination prompted; when a consultation of certain wise old ladies of the neighbourhood was held, and, after due deliberation, a bold step was decided upon against the enemy. On a Sabbath, after the conclusion of the afternoon service, some fifteen or twenty ladies, of the most knowing class, proceeded direct from the church to the house of the lunatic, and the good deacon of the parish also made it in his way to be present. What sort of amulet or charm each buxom dame wore about her person, does not appear; but the deacon took special care to be duly fortified against the wiles of the adversary, by a miniature copy of the Bible snugly stowed away in one pocket, and a book of psalms in the other. On assembling together at the house, a long and interesting conversation ensued on the subject of witchcraft and evil spirits in general, each one present having some striking illustration to offer in support of the common opinion. The deacon was especially eloquent in denouncing the wickedness of all such as sold themselves to the evil one, for the purpose of tormenting their fellow creatures, and brought up as many instances of their ultimate detection and miserable end as served to heighten the faith of all present in the success of their immediate undertaking.

The form and particulars of the whole ceremony having been settled, operations were now commenced. A huge blazing fire was kindled in the fireplace, which, by the way, was one of those old-fashioned, wide, and capacious fireplaces which would take in, at a single mouthful, the whole of a New York 'load' of wood; after which, the most ominous silence was preserved by all present, who were waiting until the last rays of the setting sun had been lost among the shadows of evening. At the proper time, on a concerted signal, the carcase of a lamb, which had just been slain, and its heart and entrails laid open, was brought into the room; the heart of which was immediately stuck full of pins, and the body then placed upon the fire, where it was consumed. The sick man, during all this process, was locked in a distant room, and one or more of the party set to watch his emotions through the keyhole of the door, during the time occupied in the sacrifice. This ceremony and sacrifice, however, proved utterly fruitless. There was no change for the better in the condition of the lunatic.

A few days after this, he commenced employing himself in walking back and forth constantly across the dooryard in front of his house. This practice he continued for weeks, following it all the day, and only prevented during the night by the interference of the family, who literally forced him into the house, until he had worn his path as smooth and uniform as the pavement. It so happened that, among the fowls of the barnyard, was a veteran old bruiser, who, from his many battles and bloody encounters, his perpetual strut and gabble, had become the acknowledged leader of his flock. No one was even bold enough to 'follow in his footsteps'. This old turkey-cock, observing the daily walk of his master, took it into his sapient head to follow his example; and it is a fact, that for days and weeks the old turkey-cock continued to walk by the side of the lunatic, facing about whenever he did, and imitating, as far as possible, his steps. The family drove him away repeatedly, though against the entreaties of the lunatic, and once shut him up for a whole week, with the design to break off the singular connection, but all to no purpose. The moment the turkey was let loose, he again entered the course with his master, and walked as long as he did.

Here was food for the lovers of the marvellous. Men, women, and children came from a great distance, to see the lunatic and his turkey. Frequent councils were held on the subject; and it was at length solemnly decided that the turkey should suffer death. He was accordingly soon afterwards beheaded, and his body submitted to the flames. Still the poor lunatic grew no better; on the contrary, he had formed a sort of attachment for the companion of his walks, and bitterly lamented his loss.

The experiments of good dames of the neighbourhood, however, did not stop here. They resolved on one more trial to exorcise the fiend. They accordingly again assembled at the house of the lunatic, with the deacon at their head. The physician was sent for, and on his arrival, he observed that an unusual number of persons were assembled. He noticed also that a brisk fire was blazing in the oven, and that the most reserved manner was adopted by all the circle around. Passing into the sick man's room, and examining his situation, he determined on bleeding him, after having been urgently pressed to do so by several of the family. After attending to this operation, he handed over the vessel containing the blood to one of the company. The physician concluded to watch by the bedside of his patient during the night. In the course of two or three hours after the bleeding, he was roused from a doze into which he had fallen, by a loud report, as of a loaded musket, in the adjoining room; and, on going out, discovered a thick smoke issuing from the mouth of the oven, and extending itself in black wreaths upward, and along the ceiling. There sat the good deacon, with Bible open upon his knees; and some half-score of old ladies were seated in grim silence around the room. On inquiring the cause of this singular scene, the doctor ascertained that the blood of the lunatic, which a few hours before he had taken from his arm, had been poured into an earthen jar, which was then hermetically sealed, and covered with small pieces of silver; and after which it was placed in the oven. As soon as the contents of the jar became sufficiently rarified, it exploded, with the effects above stated.

For a long while after this, the old ladies who officiated on this singular occasion used to tell of the strange noises they heard overhead on that night; and some of them actually believed they had got the better of the adversary, especially as it soon became noised abroad, that an old woman living in an adjoining town, and long suspected of witchcraft, actually died on that eventful night. The poor lunatic, however, was never the better for these kind but mistaken efforts on his behalf, and in a few months he died.

IX

THE SEVERED ARM
Or, The Wehr-wolf of Limousin
Anonymous

In my previous study of the Gothic genre, *Great Tales of Terror
from Europe and America* (1972), I presented what I then believed to be the earliest short story about a werewolf—a tale entitled "Huges, The Wehr-Wolf" by one Sutherland Menzies, which
had first appeared in an American magazine in 1838. I noted that
it pre-dated by a whole year what until then had been thought
to be the first short story of such a creature, "The White Wolf
of the Hartz Mountains", which is actually an episode from
Captain Marryat's novel, *The Phantom Ship*, but often reprinted
on its own. However, my research among the 'bluebooks' now
causes me to overturn that claim with a still earlier story, "The
Severed Arm; Or, The Wehr-Wolf of Limousin", which un-
fortunately I cannot date exactly, but is certainly *circa* 1820—
some eighteen years earlier than the previous claimant! I found
the story in a collection entitled *Tales of Superstition*, published by
Dean & Munday of Threadneedle Street, another London firm
who put out a great many 'Shilling Shockers'. For once the book
was decorated with a rather innocuous engraving of a knight in
armour starting back from a wan-looking ghost, but the tales which
the anonymous writer had assembled about phantoms, demons,
fairies and some monsters of legend made interesting and often
exciting reading. But it was the werewolf tale, "The Severed Arm",
that obviously caught my eye, and in both style and quality it far
surpasses the rest; indeed I am tempted to conjecture that it may
have been lifted from another source. In any event, it is clearly
the first of its kind and a most important addition to the canon
of werewolf stories.

*   *   *

THE ANCIENT PROVINCE of Poictou, in France, has long been celebrated in the annals of romance, as one of the most famous haunts of those dreadful animals, whose species is between a phantom and a beast of prey; and which are called by Germans, wehr-wolves, and by the French, Bisclavarets, or Loups Garoux. To the English, these midnight terrors are yet unknown, and almost without a name; but when they are spoken of in this country they are called, by the way of eminence, wild wolves. The common superstition concerning them is, that they are men in compact with the arch enemy, who have the power of assuming the form and nature of wolves at certain periods.

The hilly and woody district of the Upper Limousin, which now forms the southern division of the Upper Vienne, was that particular part of the province which the wehr-wolves were supposed to inhabit: whence, like the animal which gave them their name, they would wander out by midnight, far from their own hills and mountains, and run howling through the silent streets of the nearest towns and villages, to the great terror of all the inhabitants; whose piety however, was somewhat increased by these supernatural visitations.

There once stood in the suburbs of the town of St Yrieux, which is situate in those dangerous parts of ancient Poictou, an old, but handsome *Maison-de-Plaisance*, or, in plain English, a countryhouse, belonging, by ancient descent, to the young Baroness Louise Joliedame; who, out of dread to the terrible Wehr-Wolves, a well-bred horror at the *chambres à l'antique* which it contained, and a greater love for the gallant court of Francis I, let the chateau to strangers; though they occupied but a very small portion of it, whilst the rest was left unrepaired, and was rapidly passing to decay. One of the parties by whom the old mansion was tenanted, was a country chirurgeon, named Antoine du Pilon; who (according to his own account) was not only well acquainted with the science of Galen and Hippocrates, but was also a profound adept in those arts, for the learning of which some men toil their whole lives away, and are none the wiser; such as alchemy, converse with spirits, magic, and so forth. Dr du Pilon had abundant leisure to talk of his knowledge at the cabaret of St Yrieux, which bore the sign of the Chevalier Bayard's arms, where he assembled round him many of the idler members of the town, the chief of whom were Cuirbouilli, the currier; Malbois, the joiner; La Jacquette, the tailor; and Nicole Bonvarlet, his host; together with several other equally arrant gossips, who all swore roundly, at the end of their parleys, that Dr Antoine du Pilon was the best doctor, and the wisest man in the whole world! To remove, however, any wonder that may arise in the reader's mind how a professor of such skill and knowledge should be left to waste his abilities so remote from the patronage of the great, it should be remarked, that in such cases as had already come before him, he had not been quite so successful as could have been expected or desired, since old Genefrede Corbeau, who was frozen almost double with age and ague, he kept cold and fasting to preserve her from fever; and he would have cut off the leg of Pierre Faucile, the reaper, when he wounded his right arm in the harvest time, to prevent his flesh from mortifying downwards!

In a retired apartment of the same deserted mansion where this mirror of chirargeons resided, dwelt a peasant, and his daughter, who had come to St Yrieux from a distant part of Normandy, and of whose history nothing was known, but that they seemed to be in the deepest poverty; although they neither asked relief, nor uttered a single complaint. Indeed, they rather avoided all discourse with their gossiping neighbours, and even with their fellow inmates, excepting so far as the briefest courtesy required; and as they were able, on entering their abode, to place a reasonable security for payment in the hands of old Gervais, the Baroness Joliedame's steward, they were permitted to live in the old chateau with little questioning, and less sympathy. The father appeared in general to be a plain, rude peasant, whom poverty had somewhat tinctured with misanthropy: though there were times when his bluntness towered into a haughtiness not accordant with his present station, but seemed like a relique of a higher sphere, from which he had fallen. He strove, and the very endeavour increased the bitterness of his heart to mankind, to conceal his abject indigence; but that was too apparent to all, since he was rarely to be found at St Yrieux, but led a wild life in the adjacent mountains and forests, occasionally visiting the town to bring to his daughter Adele a portion of the spoil, which as a hunter, he indefatigably sought for the subsistence of both. Adele, on the contrary, though she felt as deeply as her father the sad reverse of fortune to which they were exposed, had more gentleness in her sorrow, and more content in her humiliation. She would, when he returned to the cottage, worn with the fatigue of his forest labours, try, but many times in vain, to bring a smile to his face and consolation to his heart. "My father," she would say, "quit, I beseech you, this wearisome hunting for some safer employment nearer home. You depart, and I watch in vain for your return; days and nights pass away, and you come not!— while my disturbed imagination will ever whisper the danger of a forest midnight, fierce howling wolves, and robbers still more cruel."

"Robbers! girl, sayest thou?" answered her father with a bitter laugh, "and what shall they gain from me, think ye? Is there aught in this worn-out gaberdine to tempt them? Go to, Adele! I am not now Count Gaspar de Marcanville, the friend of the royal Francis, and a knight of the Holy Ghost; but plain Hubert, the Hunter of the Limousin; and wolves, thou trowest, will not prey upon wolves."

"But, my dearest father," said Adele, embracing him, "I would that thou wouldst seek a safer occupation nearer to our dwelling, for I would be by your side."

"What wouldst have me to do, girl?" interrupted Gaspar impatiently; "wouldst have me put this hand to the sickle or the plough, which has so often grasped a sword in the battle, and a banner-lance in the tournament? Or shall a companion of Le Saint Esprit become a fellow-hand-worker with the low artisans of this miserable town? I tell thee, Adele, that but for thy sake I would never again quit the forest, but would remain there in a savage life, till I forgot my language and my species, and become a wehrwolf or a wild buck!"

Such was commonly the close of their conversation; for if Adele dared to press her entreaties further, Gaspar, half frenzied, would not fail to call to her mind all the unhappy circumstances of his fall, and work himself almost to madness by their repetition. He had, in early life, been introduced by the Count de Saintefleur to the court of Francis I, where he had risen so high in the favour of his sovereign, that he was continually in his society; and in the many wars which so embittered the reign of that excellent monarch, de Marcanville's station was ever by his side. In these conflicts, Gaspar's bosom had often been the shield of Francis even in moments of the most imminent danger; and the grateful king as often showered upon his deliverer those rewards which, to the valiant and high-minded soldier, are far dearer than riches— the glittering jewels of knighthood, and the golden coronal of the peerage. To that friend who had fixed his feet so loftily and securely in the slippery paths of a court, Gaspar felt all the ardour of youthful gratitude; and yet he sometimes imagined, that he could perceive an abatement in the favour of de Saintefleur as that of Francis increased. The truth was, that the gold and rich promises of the king's great enemy, the Emperor Charles V, had induced de Saintefleur to swerve from his allegiance; and he now waited but for a convenient season to put the darkest designs in practice against his sovereign. He also felt no slight degree of envy, even against that very person whom he had been the instrument of raising; and at length an opportunity occurred, when he might gratify both his ambition and his revenge by the same blow. It was in one of those long wars in which the French monarch was engaged, and in which de Saintefleur and de Marcanville were his constant companions, that they were both watching his couch while he slept, when the former, in a low tone of voice, thus began to sound the faith of the latter to his royal master.

"What sayest thou, Gaspar, were not a prince's coronet and a king's revenue in Naples, better than thus ever-toiling in a war that seems unending? Hearest thou, brave de Marcanville? We can close it with the loss of one life only!"

"Queen of Heaven!" ejaculated Gaspar, "what is it thou wouldst say, de Saintefleur?"

"Say! why that there have been other kings in France before this Francis, and will be, when he shall have gone to his place. Thinkest thou that he of the double-headed black eagle, would not amply reward the sword that cut this fading lily from the earth?"

"No more, no more, de Saintefleur," cried Gaspar; "even from you who placed me where I might flourish beneath the lily's shade, will I not hear this treason. Rest secure that I will not betray thee to the king; my life shall sooner be given for thine; but I will watch thee with more vigilance than the wolf hath when he watcheth the night-fold, and your first step to the heart of Francis shall be over the body of Gaspar de Marcanville."

"Nay, then," said de Saintefleur, aside, "he must be my first victim"; and immediately drawing his sword, he cried aloud, "What, ho! guards! treason!"—whilst Gaspar stood immovable with astonishment and horror. The event is soon related; for Francis was but too easily persuaded that de Marcanville was in reality guilty of the act about to be perpetrated by de Saintefleur; and the magnanimity of Gaspar was such, that not one word which might criminate his former friend could be drawn from him, even to save his own life. The kind-hearted Francis, however, was unable to forget in a moment the favour with which for years he had been accustomed to look upon de Marcanville; and it was only at the earnest solicitation of the courtiers, many of whom were rejoiced at the thought of a powerful rival's removal, that he could be prevailed on to pass upon him even the sentence of degradation and banishment.

Gaspar hastened to his chateau, but the treasures which he was allowed to bear with him into exile, were little more than his wife Rosalie and his daughter Adele; with whom he immured himself in the dark and almost boundless recesses of the Hanoverian Hartz, where his sorrows soon rendered his gaunt and attenuated form altogether unknown. In this savage retirement he drew up a faithful narration of de Saintefleur's treachery; and, in confirmation of its truth, procured a certificate from his confessor, Father Ægidius— one of those holy men, who of old were dwellers in forests and deserts—and directing it "To the King", placed it in the hands of his wife, that if, in any of those hazardous excursions in which he was engaged to procure their daily subsistence, he should perish, it might be delivered to Francis, and his family thus be restored to their rank and estates, when his pledge to de Saintefleur could no longer be claimed. Years passed away, and, in the gloomy recesses of the Hercynian woods, Gaspar acquired considerable skill as a hunter; had it been to preserve his own life only, he had laid him down calmly upon the sod, and resigned that life to famine, or to the hungry wolf; but he had still two objects which bound him to existence, and therefore in the chase the wild buck was too slow to escape his spear, and the bear too weak to resist his attacks.

His fate, notwithstanding, preyed heavily upon him, and he often broke out in fits of vehement passion, and the most bitter lamentations; which at length so wrought upon the grief-worn frame of Rosalie de Marcanville, that about ten years after Gaspar's exile, her death left him a widower, when his daughter Adele was scarcely eighteen years of age. It was then, with a mixture of desperation and distress, that de Marcanville determined to rush forth from his solitude into France; and, careless of the fate which might await him for returning from exile unrecalled, to advance even to the court, and laying his papers at the foot of the throne, to demand the ordeal of combat with de Saintefleur; but when he had arrived at the woody province of Upper Limousin, his purpose failed him, as he saw in the broad daylight, which rarely entered the Hartz Forest, the afflicting changes which ten years of the severest labour, and the most heartfelt sorrow, had made upon his form. He might, indeed, so far as it regarded all recollections of his person, have safely gone even into the court of Francis; but Gaspar also saw, that in the retired forest surrounding St Yrieux, he might still reside unknown to his beloved France; that under the guise of a hunter, he could still provide for the support of his gentle Adele; and that, in the event of his death he should be considerably nearer to the sovereign's abode. It was then, in consequence of these reasons, that de Marcanville employed a part of his small remaining property, in securing a residence in the dilapidated chateau, as it has been already mentioned.

It was some time after their arrival, that the inhabitants of the town of St Yrieux were alarmed by the intelligence that a wehr-wolf, or perhaps a troop of them, certainly inhabited the woods of Limousin. The most terrific howlings were heard in the night, and the wild rush of a chase swept through the deserted streets; yet the townspeople—according to the most approved rules for acting where wehr-wolves are concerned—never once thought of sallying forth in a body, and with weapons and lighted brands, to scare the monsters from their prey; but adding a more secure fastening to every window, which is the wehr-wolf's usual entrance, they deserted such as had already fallen their victims, with one brief expression of pity for them, and many a "Dieu et benit!" for themselves. It was asserted, too, that some of the country people, whose dwellings came more immediately into contact with the Limousin forests, had lost their children; whose lacerated remains, afterwards discovered in the woods, only half devoured, plainly denoted them to have fallen the prey of some abandoned wehr-wolf!

It is not surprising, that in a retired town, where half the people were without employment, and all were thoroughbred gossips, and lovers of wonders, that the inroads of the wehr-wolf formed too important an epoch in their history, to be passed over without a due discussion. Under pretence, therefore, of being a protection to each other, many of the people of St Yrieux, and especially the worthy conclave mentioned at the beginning of this history, were almost eternally convened at the Chevalier Bayard's Arms, talking over their nightly terrors, and filling each other with such affright, by the repetition of many a lying old tale upon the same subject, that, too much alarmed to part, they often agreed to pass the night over Nicole Bonvarlet's wine flask and blazing faggots. Upon a theme so intimately connected with a magical lore as is the history of wehr-wolves, Dr Antoine du Pilon discoursed like a Solomon; citing, to the great edification and wonder of his hearers, such hosts of authors, both sacred and profane, that he who should have hinted, that the wehr-wolves of St Yrieux were simply like other wolves, would have found as little gentleness in his hearers as he would have experienced from the animals themselves.

*   *   *

"Well, my masters?" began Bonvarlet, one evening when they were met, "I would not, for a tun of malmsey wine now, be in the Limousin forest tonight; for do ye hear how it blusters and pours? By the ship of St Mildred, in a wild night like this, there is no place in the world like your hearthside in a goodly submerge, with a merry host and good liquor; both of which, neighbours, ye have to admiration."

"Ay, Nicole," replied Courbouilli, "it is a foul night, truly, either for man or cattle; and yet I'll warrant ye that the wehr-wolves will be out in it, for their skin is said to be the same as that the fiend himself wears, and that would shut you out water, and storm, and wind, like a castle wall."

"Hark, neighbours, did ye hear that cry? It is a wehr-wolf's bark!" exclaimed Jerome Malbois, starting from his settle.

"Ay, by the bull of St Luke, did I, friend, Jerome," returned Bonvarlet; "surely the great fiend himself can make no worse a howling; I even thought 'twould split the very rafters last night, though I deem they're of good seasoned fir."

"There is the cry again!" exclaimed Malbois, and as the sounds drew nearer, the doctor's audience evinced symptoms of alarm, which were rapidly increasing, when a still louder shriek was heard close to the house.

"What ho, within there!" cried a voice, evidently of one in an agony of terror, "an ye be men, open the door," and the next moment it was burst from its fastenings by the force of a human body falling against it, which dropped without motion upon the floor.

The confusion which this accident created may well be imagined; the doctor, greatly alarmed, retreated into the fireplace, whence he cried out to the equally scared rustics, "It's a wehr-wolf in a human shape; don't touch him, I tell you, but strike him with a fire fork between the eyes, and he'll turn to a wolf and run away."

"Peace, Doctor," said Bonvarlet, the only one of the party who had ventured near the stranger; "he breathes yet, for he's a Christian man like as we are; so come, you prince of all chirurgeons, and bleed him; and when he comes to, why school him yourself."

The doctor advanced from his retreat, with considerable reluctance, to attend upon his patient, who was richly habited in the luxuriant fashion of the court of Francis, and appeared to be a middle-aged man, of handsome features, and commanding presence. As the doctor, somewhat reassured, began to remove the short cloak to find out the stranger's arm, he started back with affright, and actually roared with pain at receiving a deep scratch from the huge paw of a wolf, which apparently grew out from his shoulder. "Avaunt thee, Sathanas!" ejaculated the doctor, "I told thee how it would be, my masters, that this cursed wehr-wolf would bleed us first. By the porker of St Anthony! Blessed beast! See he hath clawed me from the biceps flexor cubiti, down to the Os Lunare, even as a peasant would plough over a furrow!"

"Ha, ha, ha," laughed Bonvarlet, holding up the dreaded wolf's paw, which was yet bleeding, as if it had been recently separated from the animal. "Here is no wehr-wolf, but a brave hunter, who hath cut off his goodly forepaw in the forest, with his couteau-de-chasse; but soft," he added, throwing it aside, "he recovers!"

"Pierre!—Henri!" said the stranger, recovering, "where are ye? How far is the king behind us? Ha, what place is this? And who are ye?" he continued, looking round.

"This, your good worship, is the Chevalier Bayard's Arms, in the town of St Yrieux, where your honour fell, through loss of blood, as I guess, by this wound. We were fain to keep the door barred for fear of the wehr-wolves; and we half deemed your lordship to be one, at first sight of the great paw you carried, but now I judge you brought it from the forest."

"Ay! yes, thou art in the right on't," said the stranger, recollecting himself. "I was in the forest! I tell thee, host, that I have this night looked upon the arch demon himself!"

"Away, Lucifer!" ejaculated the doctor, devoutly crossing his breast; "and have I received a claw from his forefoot? I feel the enchantment of lycanthropy coming over me; I shall be a wehr-wolf myself, shortly; for what saith Hornhoofius, in his Treatise de Diabolus, lib. xiv. cap. xxiii. They who are torn by a wehr-wolf—Oh me!—Oh me!—Libera nos Domine. Look to yourselves, neighbours, or I shall raven upon ye all."

"I pray you, Master Doctor," said Bonvarlet, "to let his lordship tell us his story first, and then we'll hear yours.—How was it, fair sir?—but take another cup of wine first."

"My tale is brief," answered the stranger: "The king is passing tonight through the Limousin, and with two of his attendants I rode forward to prepare for his coming; when, in the darkness of the wood, we were separated, and, as I galloped on alone, an enormous wolf, with fiery flashing eyes, leaped out of a brake before me, with the most fearful howlings, and rushed on me with the speed of lightning. As the wolf leaped upon my horse, I drew my couteau-de-chasse, and severed that huge paw which you found upon me: but as the violence of the blow made the weapon fall, I caught up a large forked branch of a tree, and struck the animal upon the forehead: upon which, my horse began to rear and plunge; for, where the wolf stood, I saw by a momentary glimpse of moonlight the form of an ancient enemy, who had long since been banished from France, and whom I believed to have died of famine in the Hartz Forest."

"Look you there now," said du Pilon, "a blow between the eyes with a forked stick—said I not so from Philo-Diamones, lib. xcii? Oh, I'm condemned to be a wehr-wolf of a verity, and I shall eat those of my most intimate acquaintances the first. Masters look to yourselves:—O dies infelix! Oh unhappy man that I am!"—and with these words he rushed out of the cottage.

"I think the very fiend is in Monsieur the Doctor, tonight," cried the host, "for here he's gone off without dressing his honour's wounds."

"Heed not that, friend, but do thou provide torches and assistance to meet the king; my wound is but small; but when my horse saw the apparition I told you of, he bounded forward like a wild Russian colt, dragged me through all the briers of the forest —for there seemed a troop of a thousand wolves howling behind us—and at the verge of it he dropped lifeless, and left me, still pursued, to gain the town, weak and wounded as I was."

"St Dennis be praised now!" said Bonvarlet, "you showed a good heart, my lord; but we'll at once set out to meet the king; so neighbours take each of ye a good pine faggot off the hearth, and call up more help as you go; and Nicolette and Madeline will prepare for our return."

"But," asked the stranger, "where's the wolf's paw that I brought from the forest?"

"I cast it aside, my lord," answered Bonvarlet, "till you had recovered; but I would fain beg it of you as a gift, for I will hang it over my fireplace, and have its story made into a song by Rowland the minstrel—and, mother of God! What is this?" continued he, putting into his guest's hand a human arm, cut off at the elbow, vested in the worn-out sleeve of a hunter's coat, and bleeding freshly at the part where it was dissevered.

"Holy St Mary!" exclaimed the stranger, regarding the hand attentively, "this is the arm of Gaspar de Marcanville, yet bearing the executioner's brand burnt in his flesh; and he is a wehr-wolf!"

"Why," said Bonvarlet, "that's the habit worn by the melancholy hunter, whose daughter lives at the chateau yonder. He rarely comes to St Yrieux, but when he does, he brings more game than any ten of your gentlemen huntsmen ever did. Come, we'll go seek the daughter of this man-wolf, and then on to the forest, for this fellow deserves a stake and a bundle of faggots, as well as ever Jeanne d'Arc did, in my simple thinking."

They then proceeded to Adele, at the dilapidated chateau; and her distress at the foregoing story may better be conceived than described; yet she offered not the slightest resistance to accompanying them to the forest; but when one of the party mentioned their expected meeting with the king, her eyes became suddenly lighted up, and retiring for a moment, she expressed herself in readiness to attend them. At the skirts of the forest they found an elderly man, of a strange, quaint appearance, crouching in the fern like a hare, who called out to them, in a squeaking voice, that was at once familiar to all, "Take care of yourselves, good people, for I am a wehr-wolf, and shall speedily spring upon ye."

"Why, that's our doctor, as I am a sinful man," cried Bonvarlet; "let's try his own cure upon him. Neighbour Malbois, give me a tough forked branch, and I'll disenchant him, I warrant; and you, Courboulli, out with your knife, as though you would skin him"— and then he continued aloud, "Oh, honest friend, you're a wehr-wolf, are you? Why, then, I'll dispossess the devil that's in you. You shall be flayed, and then burnt for a wizard."

With that the rustics of St Yrieux, who enjoyed the jest, fell upon the unhappy doctor, and, by a sound beating, and other rough usage, so convinced him that he was not a wehr-wolf, that he cried out, "Praised be St Gregory, I am a whole man again. Lo, I am healed, but my bones feel wondrous sore! Who is he that hath cured me?—By the mass, I am grievously bruised!—Thanks to the seraphical Father Francis, the devil hath gone out of me!"

Whilst the peasants were engaged in searching for the king's party and the mutilated wolf, the stranger who was left with Adele de Marcanville, fainted through loss of blood; and, as she bent over him, and stanched his wounds with her scarf, he said, with a faint voice—"Fair one, who is it, thinkest thou, whom thou art so blessedly attending?"

"I wot not," answered she, "but that thou art a man."

"Hear me, then, and throw aside these bandages for my dagger, for I am thy father's ancient enemy, the Count de Saintefleur."

"Heaven forgive you then," returned Adele, "for the time of vengeance belongs to it only."

"And it is come!" cried a loud hoarse voice, as a large wolf, wounded by the loss of a forepaw, leaped upon the count and put an end to his existence. At the same moment, the royal train, which the peasants had discovered, rode up with flambeaux, and a knight, with a large partisan, made a blow at the wolf, whom Adele vainly endeavoured to preserve, since the stroke was of sufficient power to destroy both. The wolf gave one terrific howl, and fell backwards in the form of a tall gaunt man, in a hunting dress; whilst Adele, drawing a packet from her bosom, and offering it to the king, sank lifeless upon the body of her father, Gaspar de Marcanville, the wehr-wolf of Limousin.

X

FIVE HUNDRED YEARS HENCE!

by 'D'

I have to admit now that when I was carrying out my research among the 'bluebooks' still extant in the British Museum, the University of London Library, and a few private collections in Britain, one of the very last things I ever expected to find was a story of science fiction. Yet, "Five Hundred Years Hence!", the last item in this collection, can really only be categorised as such, for it is a quite remarkable essay written in 1818 predicting what life will be like in the year 2318. The piece came to light in a publication, *The Pocket Magazine*, from the firm of John Arliss. (Arliss, you will recall, was the publisher of Sarah Wilkinson's "The Mysterious Novice", the second story in the book.) 'Bluebooks' carrying the title of 'magazines' are not altogether uncommon, and they are in the main collections of stories and "Gothic anecdotes of freaks, monsters and murders" to quote the authority, William Watt. The item in question, however, was seemingly sent to the publishers by a contributor who signed himself 'D', and it is prefaced by the following remarks: "I have ventured to send you the following. It is written as a peep into futurity, under the idea that if England, France and Europe generally have risen, and Egypt, Turkey and Asia have fallen, England and the surrounding states may fall, and their glory retire more westward, as that of the eastern parts have done; and thus America, in the end, rise to the splendour of a midday sun. However improbable this may seem, yet we have example before us, and I think it may form an amusing speculation." Naturally, I read the item with mounting fascination and likewise the editor's comments upon it at the end. Having finished, I worked my way on through later issues of *The Pocket Magazine* in the hope that the ingenious 'D' had felt inclined to speculate further. I was not disappointed, for not only had he taken up his pen to defend his ideas against the attack of the editor, but added several more visionary suggestions that by 2318 man would have discovered perpetual motion, invented a universal language, journeyed inside the earth and reached the moon! I do not wish to spoil the reader's enjoyment of "Five Hundred Years Hence!" by saying any more, but it is a most fitting item with which to end this anthology and surely provides, in company with my other selections, a most emphatic denial of frequently voiced opinion that the 'bluebook'—the much abused 'Shilling Shocker'—contained "nothing original".

*   *   *

LONDON, OCTOBER 1, 2318.—This place, once a metropolis, but now an obscure village, is daily becoming less in the estimation of its inhabitants and its neighbours. The small fishing trade, which is now the only trade exercised here, is incompetent to support much longer the few people who reside here. There is no other resource, as the ground, for many miles round, cannot be cultivated, it being all a complete heap of ruins. There were found here lately a few of the coins of George III called, at that time, sovereigns and regents. They are considered by the curious as being well worth attention, as they involve much speculative opinion, relative to the cause of our present low station in the scale of nations. One ballad press does all the printing required to be executed here.

OXFORD, OCTOBER 1, 2318.—This place, once a university, and a large, extensive, and flourishing town, has dwindled, year by year, to its present insignificance. Yesterday there arrived here three students, to the only one college remaining, and, we are sorry to say, it is expected no more will come this season. This is not much to be wondered at, as the sight of colleges desolate, inhabitants fled, and every part of the town showing that the prosperity of the country had long since been at its meridian, and is now sinking into oblivion, is no very interesting prospect, or enticement for young men, to those studies which flourish as a country flourishes.

LIVERPOOL, OCTOBER 1, 2318.—Two vessels, laden with the produce of Spain, touched here for water a few days since. These are the only vessels which have been sent here for above a month.

EDINBURGH, OCTOBER 1, 2318.—Last week, by a special order from the government, three men were executed in the new way (by hanging with their heads downwards), for having the daring impudence to assert, in the open street, in public violation of respect for the three great kings, that "America was the only country for liberty, and England was becoming desolate". They appeared resigned, but did not seem sorry for what they had done. They died in two hours and twenty-nine minutes.

PHILADELPHIA, OCTOBER 1, 2318.—This city, now so flourishing, lately added, by an act of the assembly, thirteen new parishes, all of which are extremely well built, and every house has the excellent recommendation of being slated with iron. The population of this place, and suburbs, has been computed lately, and is stated at two millions souls. The markets here are kept in the strictest order, and no filth is seen about the streets. The method of keeping the markets clean we recommend to general notice. The wagons with ten wheels are used for this purpose; and, as they pass through the markets every hour, the people throw into them all waste whatever. For this purpose a small tax is levied, which the inhabitants pay with pleasure, as it conduces so much to their own comfort.

WASHINGTON, OCTOBER 1, 2318.—This large city, which was called after the name, and in honour of a warrior, who lived more than six centuries ago, is now in the most flourishing state. We need scarcely mention more than the size of it. It, at this time, covers forty square miles, and being built on its original plan, of a garden to every house, it affords the best possible convenience to the inhabitants. There are three monuments here, to the memory of General Washington, and his contemporary, that eminent philosopher and statesman, Benjamin Franklin. These are erected, to remind the citizens of the means they used for freedom and independence.

NEW YORK, OCTOBER 1, 2318.—The progress of literature, which has been attended to so little for such a length of time, is now much encouraged. Upon an average, there are forty new works published every week in this city. There are twenty daily, and forty weekly newspapers. It may be a matter of some surprise, from whence materials arrive to form such an amazing expenditure (if it may be so called) of literary matter; but when it is considered that England, France, and the whole of the eastern territory, have been falling for many ages, this idea will furnish much speculation; and when we consider, that in this country genius is everywhere encouraged, to an extent that the barbarous ages of English superiority never knew, this will redeem us, in some measure, from a charge of improbability.

The curious works printed some four or five hundred years ago, are objects of great curiosity among the connoisseurs of the day. The mathematical uprightness of the roman type then in use, and the curious inclination of the italic, form an amusing companion with the works of the day; as, of course, our prevailing letter leans the contrary way to the italic of former times. These are sufficient to denote the barbarous state of the arts at that period.

OBSERVATIONS ON THE PRECEDING ARTICLE

Such predictions as those of our correspondent have often been hazarded; but we are strongly disposed to think that they will not be verified by time. We believe that the celebrated Bishop Berkeley was one of the first, if not the first, of the prophets on this subject. There are some lines of his, four of which, if we remember right (for we quote from memory), are as follows:

> "Westward the scene of empire bends its way:
>   The first four acts already past,
> The fifth shall close the drama with the day!
>   Time's noblest offspring is his last."

Since the period when Bishop Berkeley lived, the prediction has been often repeated. We have somewhere seen, but we cannot immediately point out where, a paper ·of much the same kind as that which we now insert from our ingenious correspondent. Like his, it goes on the supposition that the glory of Britain is at an end, and that of America shining with super-lative splendour. That the American continent will hold a dis-tinguished rank in the civilised world, there can be little reason to doubt; but we doubt very much whether it will ultimately form that immense and overpowering empire, which some persons imagine it will. It appears to us, that long before the lapse of five centuries, perhaps even before the lapse of fifty years, the vast extent of territory between the St Lawrence, the Mississippi, and the Atlantic, will be divided into, at least, three independent states. This is, indeed, in the natural order of things. There is no strong natural bond of union between the Northern, the Southern, and the Trans-Alleghenian States. Between the manners, habits, and pursuits of the New England and the Southern States there is a striking difference. The Western States are bound by a feeble tie to the rest of the American confederacy. The whole must, inevitably, be split into fractions on some future day. Nor do we think that this disjunction will be injurious to the happiness of the Americans themselves. We sincerely hope that it will not. Much as we dislike some parts of their character, we trust that they will be a flourishing and a happy people.

With respect to our native country, we cannot give our assent to the opinion, that it must necessarily decline. Whatever defects there may be in some of its institutions, and we are not blind to those defects, we are convinced that it possesses an inherent, everduring energy and spirit, which will preserve it from sinking into the wretched decrepitude, which is now the lot of many nations that formerly were great. It would, perhaps, not be difficult to show, that the causes which brought about the ruin of the ancient states, neither do, nor can exist for us. It has been a favourite practice with many persons, to draw a comparison between kingdoms and individuals, and to infer that the one, as well as the other, must necessarily pass through all the various stages, from infancy to extinction. But, on this question, we entirely agree with the sentiments which Mr Burke has elegantly expressed, in the opening of his first Letter on a Regicide Peace. "I am not," says he, "quite of the mind of those speculators, who seem assured, that necessarily, and by the constitution of things, all states have the same periods of infancy, manhood, and decrepitude, that are found in the individuals who compose them. Parallels of this sort rather furnish similitudes to illustrate or to adorn, than to supply analogies from whence to reason. The objects which are attempted to be forced into an analogy, are not found in the same classes of existence. Individuals are physical beings, subject to laws universal and invariable. The immediate cause acting in these laws may be obscure. The general results are subjects of certain calculation.

But commonwealths are not physical, but moral essences. They are artificial combinations, and, in their proximate efficient cause, the arbitrary productions of the human mind. We are not yet acquainted with the laws which necessarily influence the stability of that kind of work, made by that kind of agent. There is not in the physical order (with which they do not appear to hold any assignable connection), a distinct cause by which any of those fabrics must necessarily grow, flourish, or decay; nor, in my opinion, does the moral world produce anything more determinate on that subject, than what may serve as an amusement (liberal indeed, and ingenious, but still only an amusement), for speculative men."

While our correspondents keep within the limits assigned by law and morality, we have no wish to restrain the flight of their genius; but we may be allowed to hint to them, that there is something ungracious, as well as gloomy, in predicting evil, and especially when that order is predicted to the land which ought to be dear to us—the land of our birth. More noble, more worthy of a true patriot, was the language of the celebrated Paolo Sarpri whose last words were a prayer for the perpetuity of the republic under which he was born, and of which he had never ceased to be not merely a faithful, but a zealous subject.—ED.

*   *   *

TO THE EDITOR OF THE POCKET MAGAZINE

MR EDITOR—I have to return thanks for your favourable reception of my last communication, "Five Hundred Years Hence!" and for its insertion, and also for your observations on the same.

Perhaps I did not sufficiently explain my *intention* in giving such a sketch of futurity—I intended it more as a speculation than a prediction. However, taking the thing in both lights, I give the following arguments for its ultimate truth. I enclose another article as a continuation, which you can either insert as such, or otherwise, as you may think fit; it was written at the time but mislaid: its object is "Future inventions and improvements".

I think it will be generally admitted, that the proper business, end, and object of human pursuit, is not, as is often supposed, happiness, or to gratify the appetites or passions, but the improvement of our whole intellectual faculties. This I could prove by argument, if I thought it necessary.

If, then, we are not to pursue the dictates of passion, because being of a nature generally contrary to reason, they act against it; we therefore must pursue passion only when it is subservient to wisdom, and wisdom for the sake of itself.

If we examine into the causes of the decline of empires, we shall find, that it has been the indulgence in ambitions, envy, pride, revenge, and the other despicable passions, which has in a great measure produced that decline; but this fluctuation has never been caused by the steady pursuit of wisdom; the errors of ages are indeed sufficient to manifest that she is the only proper pursuit.

To reduce this argument to our present purpose, we need but remark, that when a *man* pursues only that which is reasonable and right, he will ensure to himself his portion of prosperity. And to make use of analogy, and consider a kingdom as one—if the governors of a kingdom, pursue the course of reason, it will, in like manner, ensure to that kingdom, prosperity; and that prosperity will last as long as the governors pursue the course which accords with wisdom.

In this point of view, then, how do we account for the fall of empires? I answer, history affords examples numerous enough to demonstrate, that it is by the governors of nations having been hurried on by ambition, pride, avarice, revenge, cruelty, that nations have been brought to a level with barbarism. But when a contrary course is embraced, and every action of man is made subservient to his reason, then it is that nations rise, and rise never to fall!

Whether the passions, or the causes (whatever they may be) which contributed to the decline of the eastern nations, now reside amongst us, I will not determine. I may, however, repeat, that it is on the folly, weakness, and ignorance of governments, or their wisdom and energy, that the events of nations depend. And if this be the case, which will perhaps be admitted, it only remains to know, whether these faults do exist or not, to determine the *truth* of the speculation. Time, which proves most things, will also prove this; and posterity must judge of the excellence of governments by the balance of prosperity.

October 15 1818   *** D*****

INVENTIONS AND IMPROVEMENTS
FIVE HUNDRED YEARS HENCE

FREDERICK, NEW BRUNSWICK, NOVEMBER 1, 2318.—Near this place, the workmen have begun to sink an amazing pit, which is intended to investigate the interior of the earth. Whether it is hollow, as some have asserted, or whether filled with condensed air, as Dr Franklin supposed, or whether it has a regular solid strata of stone, earth, coals, clay, and the other materials which we discover on the surface, has long been an object of enquiry among intelligent men. This is the object of the present enterprise. They have now arrived to the depth of forty miles, and have discovered many metals, gems, etc. unknown before; the most prominent of which is the new metal, which from its properties is called *Hardoniensiana*, which possesses many peculiarities. Five years have already been expended in this interesting search, but the time it is intended to take is not known.

NEWCASTLE-UPON-TYNE, NOVEMBER 1, 2318.—We were witnesses lately to a bargain for a chaldron of coals, for which the buyer gave twenty pounds. They came from Ireland, and are thought a great rarity here. We understand that about four or five centuries ago, coals were as plentiful here as they are now at Cork and Dublin, and were to be bought as low as from forty to fifty shillings per chaldron! but owing to the amazing expenditure of them for machinery and gaslights, it need not be wondered that coals have become nearly annihilated here; our pits have been long exhausted. Wood is now much cultivated.

BALTIMORE, NOVEMBER 1, 2318.—JOURNEY TO THE MOON!— The late journey to the moon, which has excited so much interest, was performed in four weeks and two days. As our readers may not be possessed of the whole particulars, we will endeavour to relate them. Mr Oliver Airbuilder, and Mr James Sharpe, having examined into the nature of the inflammable matter of which balloons are composed, considered that a journey to the moon was practicable, and might be performed, by making the car considerably lighter, and supplying themselves with dense air from the earth, in case of necessity, by means of long tubes, and glass boxes, to fit the head. After supplying themselves with necessary provisions, etc. they entered the balloon, and went to the height of twenty miles, for the purpose of making experiments. Here they made but few observations, etc. further than that the air was very rare; and came down again to recruit themselves. On the 4th of April, they prepared to start for the amazing journey to the moon! And, at twelve o'clock midday, seated themselves in the car, together with provisions, fire, etc. etc. The balloon, being of a very unusual size, was with difficulty kept, though chained, to the earth; it had an outer covering, of a kind of oilcloth, to defend it, from whatever might obstruct or damage it. At two o'clock, on the 5th of April, having taken leave of all their friends, they ascended from the outskirts of this city. The balloon was seen for half an hour, and appeared like a speck in the clouds, after which it totally disappeared. It rose with amazing velocity at first, but slackened in pace as the air grew rarer. The wings, lately invented, made of a number of goose-quills, had a surprising effect in propelling and guiding the whole machine. Each of the travellers possessed the famous *longitude watch*; by which they were enabled to discover not only the time, but their situation. This watch was discovered a few months since, by Mons de la Rus; which, as it consists entirely of the new metal called *Hardoniensiana*, and possesses the wonderful property of moving with quickness, constantly without oil, attains the object of speculation in past ages, the longitude, and is a true time-teller at all seasons and degrees of heat. May 3, at half-past five, they found themselves within the moon's attraction, having been obliged to propel themselves to that body; and, at twelve precisely, descended on the surface of what was, to them, a new globe! But, judge of their surprise, on finding the inhabitants of the moon absolute madmen! Madmen, who had once inhabited the earth; and the punishment, or correction assigned for them, was to animate another body on the moon. The madmen were much astonished at seeing our travellers, and the first salutation they gave them was, simply, a knock-down blow; after which about two hundred of them jumped over the travellers one by one. To describe the persons and names of these madmen, would be satirical; suffice it to say, they found many more here than had ever been confined in madhouses. Here are neat towns building at one time, and pulling down at another; for, amongst madmen, what government can there be? A globe so desolate and comfortless our aeronauts were soon glad to quit.

They found the climate, where they descended, very mild; they noticed, that the earth makes a far more beautiful appearance than the moon does here, on account of its size. An eclipse happened whilst they remained, which was to them a novel and interesting sight. The whole surface of the moon is as smooth as a bowling-green, with, here and there, lakes of water, which are not deep. They suppose it is these lakes of water which cause the spots, and dark parts visible to us; as they could perceive, through a telescope, the boundaries of the four quarters of the earth, merely by the shaded parts. There are very heavy dews, but no clouds, which makes this part of the universe very eligible for viewing different planets. They did not stay to make many researches, finding the inhabitants so disagreeable, and choosing to leave that to more curious persons to perform; thinking they had done sufficient for mankind, by exploring, as much as they had, these hitherto un-known regions; and being dissatisfied with the treatment they experienced, they quitted the moon rather precipitately, for a planet more hospitable, which they will enjoy the more for having made a visit to another. No pen can describe the pleasure of their friends at again seeing these adventurers.

QUEBEC, NOVEMBER 1, 2318.—This place, once containing not more than five thousand inhabitants, has now increased to five hundred thousand, and is in the most flourishing condition. The amazing number of gaslights in this city makes the night as light as the day; and the gas is now generally applied to shipping. The "patent gasometer, a foot square", has induced the proprietors of wagons to use the article for the safety of carriage, etc.; and it is thought other vehicles will be lighted in a similar manner. The River St Lawrence is daily improving, and has been made con-siderably deeper by the machinery of Messrs Adamson: which is a steam-engine, acting as a drag. Stone bridges have been long out of use in this country; and twenty iron bridges, each of only one arch, have been erected over the river, in the walk of two miles. Buildings are constantly erecting on the banks a great distance from this place.

The large kaleidoscope, lately made here, deserves notice. It is one yard in diameter, and is filled with the most precious and valuable stones that are to be found. The cavity, for the reception of the stones, being half filled with water, which is sometimes coloured, the whole makes a most brilliant and delightful spectacle. It is said by some, that the kaleidoscope was invented as early as 1817 or 1818.

MEXICO, NOVEMBER 1, 2318.—The perpetual motion, which has so long been an object of philosophic enquiry, has at length been discovered. It has been found that the new metal, *Hardoniensiana*, in addition to its other extraordinary qualities, possesses the property of *never wearing out*. This has induced some mechanists of the present day to search for the perpetual motion, and they have succeeded; the consideration of the wear of all articles having induced many philosophers, of past times, to desist from the pursuit of what appeared to them only a phantom; but, such is the boast of our enlightened age, that we have been able to enlarge and improve every object of science. The perpetual motion has already been used for watches and clocks; and will, no doubt, in a short time, be made serviceable for other purposes.

VIRGINIA, NOVEMBER 1, 2318.—The attempts of our celebrated linguist towards reforming our alphabet, and bringing into use one universal language, have exceeded his most sanguine expectations. It is a language composed of the purities and originalities of all languages, and cannot fail to excite the attention of the learned.

The new-invented instrument, to imitate the human voice, has had machinery applied to it, in the manner of a barrel-organ. It is called the vocal instrument, and is used in our churches to read prayers.

We understand that the improvement of the Pacific and Atlantic goes on rapidly; we mean the immense canal which is cutting across the isthmus of ****. We have heard that it is the intention of the proprietors of this canal, to cut deep enough to admit ships of all burden. This will be the most useful and excellent passage to the Indies ever thought of; and promises to be the finest scenery of shipping merchandise in the world, and also the first mart for all kinds of commodities.

A BRIEF BIBLIOGRAPHY
OF 'SHILLING SHOCKERS'

(All titles are anonymous unless otherwise stated.)

The Abbess of St Hilda; A Dismal, Dreadful, Horrid Story! J. Ker, *c.* 1800.

Albani; Or, the Murderer of his Child. Tegg, 1803.

Alphonso And Elinor; Or, The Mysterious Discovery. J. Ker, *c.* 1800.

Angelina; Or, The Mystic Captives, by Henry Guy, London, *c.* 1800.

The Black Castle; Or, The Spectre of the Forest. Dean & Munday, *c.* 1808.

The Black Forest; Or, The Cavern of Horrors. Ann Lemoine, 1802.

The Bravo of Venice. Dean & Munday, 1810. Chapbook abridgement of M. G. Lewis's *Rugantino, the Bravo of Venice.*

The Castle of St Barnard; Or, The Captive of the Watch Tower. Langley & Belch, 1810.

Claireville Castle; Or, The History of Albert and Emma. J. Ker, *c.* 1800.

The Convent Spectre. London, *c.* 1808.

Cronstadt Castle; Or, The Mysterious Visitor. Ann Kemmish, *c.* 1815.

The Daemon of Venice. Tegg, 1810. Chapbook abridgement of *Zofloya; Or, The Moor* by Charlotte Dacre.

Douglas Castle; Or, The Cell of Mystery. London, *c.* 1810.

Fatherless Fanny; Or, Adventures of the Countess of Werdensdorf. Written by Herself. Harrild, *c.* 1810.

Fatherless Fanny; Or, A Young Lady's First Entrance Into Life. Tegg, 1819. Chapbook version of the famous novel attributed to Clara Reeve or T. P. Prest.

The Forest Phantom; Or, The Golden Crucifix. London, 1808.

Gothic Legends, a Tale of Mystery. London, 1802.

Gothic Pieces. J. Ker, 1804.

Gothic Stories. J. Ker, 1800.

Haunted Tower; Or, The Adventures of Sir Egbert De Rothsay. By Charles Giberne. R. Hunter, 1822.

The Irish Assassin, by Henry Vincent. London, *c.* 1800.

Kilverstone; Or, The Heir Restored. Lemoine, 1799.

Louisa, the Wandering Maniac. London, 1804.

Manfredi; Or, The Mysterious Hermit. G. Stevens, *c.* 1820.

The Marvellous Magazine and Compendium of Prodigies. T. Hurst, 1802. Chapbook abridgements of famous romances.

The Midnight Assassin; Or, Confessions of the Monk Rinaldi. Hurst, 1802. Chapbook version of Ann Radcliffe's *The Italian; Or, The Confessional of the Black Penitents.*

The Midnight Bell; Or, The Abbey of St Francis. London, 1811. Chapbook abridgement of *The Midnight Bell* by Francis Lathom.

The Midnight Groan, Or, The Spectre of the Chapel. London, 1808.

Midnight Horrors; Or, The Bandit's Daughter. Dean & Munday, *c.* 1807.

The Midnight Hour; Or, The Fatal Friendship. Lemoine & Roe, *c.* 1806.

The Monk; Or, Father Innocent, Abbot of the Capuchins. Tegg, 1803. One of the many chapbook versions of M. G. Lewis's novel, *The Monk.*

The Mysterious Bride; Or, The Statue Spectre. London, *c.* 1800.

The Mysterious Omen; Or, Awful Retribution. Harrild, 1812.

The Mysterious Pilgrim; Or, Fatal Duplicity. Langley & Belch, 1810.

The Mystic Tower; Or, Villainy Punished. Kaygill, *c.* 1800.

Nocturnal Visits; Or, The Mysterious Husband. London, *c.* 1800.

The Old English Baron. London, 1806. A chapbook abridgement of the Gothic novel of the same title by Clara Reeve.

Rayland Hall. London, *c.* 1810. Chapbook version of *The Old Manor House* by Charlotte Smith.

Recluse of the Wood. London, 1809.

The Round Tower; Or, A Tale of Mystery. Lemoine & Roe, 1803.

St Leance; Or, The Castle of Rugosa. Bailey, 1821.

The Secret Oath; Or, Blood-stained Dagger. Hurst. 1802.

The Sicilian Pirates; Or, The Pillar of Mystery. London, *c.* 1800.

Somerset Castle; Or, The Father and Daughter. A Tragic Tale.
Lemoine, 1804.

The Spectre Chief; Or, The Bloodstained Banner, By F. Legge.
Bailey, *c.* 1800.

The Spectre Mother; Or, The Haunted Tower. Dean & Munday,
1800.

A Tale of Mystery; Or, The Castle of Solitude. Tegg, 1803.
Plagiarism of *A Tale of Mystery* by Thomas Holcroft.

Tales of Superstition. Dean & Munday, *c.* 1820.

The Veiled Picture. Hurst, 1802. A chapbook abridgement of *The
Mysteries of Udolpho* by Ann Radcliffe.

The Village Maid; Or, The Interesting Adventures of Montsirant.
Lemoine & Roe, 1804.

The Wandering Spirit. London, 1802.

Wonderful Tales, London, 1802.

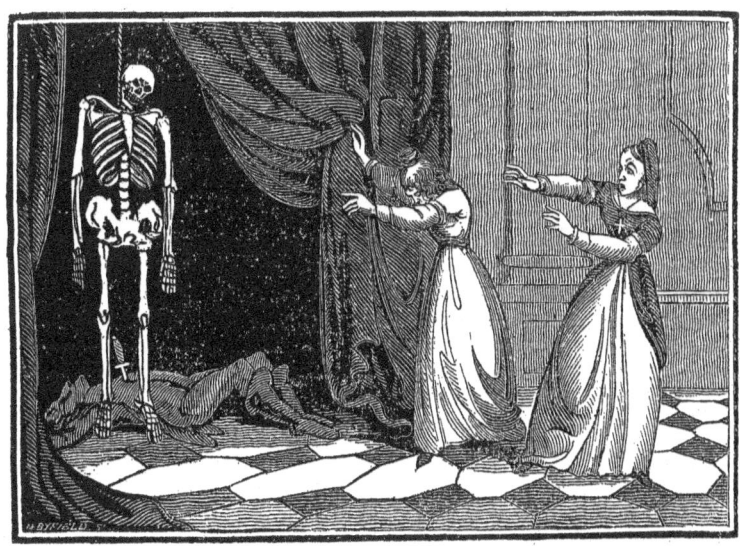

www.ingramcontent.com/pod-product-compliance
Lightning Source LLC
Chambersburg PA
CBHW020332260626
47156CB00004B/1491